OTHER NOVELS BY ROLAND SMITH

Elephant Run

Peak

Cryptid Hunters

Zach's Lie

Jack's Run

The Captain's Dog: My Journey with the Lewis and Clark Tribe

Sasquatch

Thunder Cave

Jaguar

The Last Lobo

PICTURE BOOKS WITH HIS WIFE, MARIE SMITH

B is for Beaver: An Oregon Alphabet

E is for Evergreen: A Washington State Alphabet

N is for our Nation's Capital: A Washington DC Alphabet

Z is for Zookeeper: A Zoo Alphabet

W is for Waves: An Ocean Alphabet

I, Q

(Book One: Independence Hall)

Roland Smith

Sleeping Bear Press

www.IQtheSeries.com

Copyright © 2008 Roland Smith

Library of Congress Cataloging-in-Publication Data
Smith, Roland, 1951-
I, Q : Independence Hall / written by Roland Smith.
p. cm. -- (I, Q the series)
Summary: Thirteen-year-old Q and fifteen-year-old Angela know their lives will become complicated when his mother and her father, wildly popular musicians, marry, but soon the teens are involved with spies and terrorists in Philadelphia, Pennsylvania.
[1. Spies--Fiction. 2. Terrorism--Fiction. 3. Brothers and sisters--Fiction. 4. Musicians--Fiction. 5. Remarriage--Fiction. 6. Philadelphia (Pa.)--Fiction.] I. Title.
PZ7.S65766Iab 2008
[Fic]--dc22
2008049002

ISBN 978-1-58536-325-4
10

ISBN 978-1-58536-468-8 (case)
5 7 9 10 8 6 4

This book was typeset in Berthold Baskerville and Datum
Cover design by Lone Wolf Black Sheep

Printed in the United States.

Sleeping Bear Press™

315 E. Eisenhower Parkway, Suite 200
Ann Arbor, Michigan 48108

© 2008 Sleeping Bear Press is an imprint of Gale, a part of Cengage Learning.

visit us at www.sleepingbearpress.com

Printed by Bang Printing, Brainerd, MN, 10ᵗ Ptg., 08/2011

3 9547 00396 8935

For my brother Michael
who shared his music when I was young

SUNDAY, AUGUST 31 >

From a window across the street, Eben Lavi watched the couple and the two children leave their loft and climb into the back of a white limousine. It pulled away from the curb and started down the street. A moment later a blue SUV fell in behind the limo, three cars back, and began to follow.

Eben pulled his disposable cell phone out of his pocket and thumbed in a number.

"Ziv?"

"Yes." Ziv answered from the SUV in his old, gravelly voice.

"When they get to the park, go over to San Rafael and install the device. When you're finished come back into the city. I'll call you when I'm ready to be picked up."

Eben flipped the cell phone closed and turned to the two women standing behind him. One was named Carma, the other Devorah.

"Get everything cleaned up here then get to the airport to catch your flight," Eben said. "I'm going over to the park. I'll see you in a few days."

"This is crazy," Carma said. "I say we just take her now and be done with it."

Eben pulled a light jacket over his crisp waiter's uniform and straightened his tie in the mirror. "That is my decision to make," he said calmly. "And now is not the time."

"I agree with Carma," Devorah said. "It'd be easier to take her here in San Francisco than while they're traveling."

"Not necessarily." Eben walked to the apartment door and opened it. He paused before stepping out into the hallway. "Have a good flight," he said. "I'll call you."

He closed the door and walked down the hall, wondering for the hundredth time why his superiors had decided to saddle him with two out-of-control women and an old man who should have been put out to pasture years ago.

Wedding Vows

If the ceremony didn't end soon I thought I might pass out, or worse.

"Will you, Blaze Munoz, take this man, Roger Tucker, to be your lawfully wedded husband, to have and to hold, through sickness and health, until death do you part?"

"I will."

"Will you, Roger Tucker, take this woman…"

I felt a drop of sweat dance down my side like a spider and disappear into the waistband of my itchy, brand-new suit pants, which I hoped never to wear again.

Mom, dressed in a white wedding gown, stared through her veil at her husband-to-be (my stepfather-to-be), Roger Tucker, with loving expectation. In my entire life I'd never seen this expression on Mom's face. (At least I didn't remember seeing it.)

I glanced at my future stepsister, Angela Tucker. She was staring at her dad who wore the same blissful expression as my mom. Angela looked like I felt.

"...through sickness..."

I didn't object to the marriage. In fact, I liked Roger. A lot. It was just that everything had happened so quickly.

"...and health..."

Three months ago Mom and I were living peacefully on our little sailboat in Sausalito, California, then Roger shows up at one of Mom's rare singing gigs with a pile of songs he wrote, then...

"...until death..."

They put together a band called Match and cut a single called "Rekindled." The song goes platinum in two weeks. They're signed up to record an album. They get a national tour, then...

"...do you..."

They announce their marriage, sell the sailboat, lease a bus, and sublet Roger and Angela's place in San Francisco.

"...part?"

Here it comes, I thought, trying not to sway. Mom, Roger, Angela, and me (Quest Munoz—Q for short) are heading out on a yearlong tour as soon as Roger says...

"I will."

"I now pronounce you husband and wife."

Reception

It was supposed to be a simple wedding in a small church with a little reception afterward for close friends at Roger and Angela's loft in the city.

I scanned the crowd. There were hundreds of people mingling in the roped-off Strybing Arboretum in the middle of Golden Gate Park and I didn't know more than about thirty of them. Outside the cordon, kept at bay by bicycle- and horse-mounted San Francisco police, were at least another five hundred people hoping to get a glimpse of the invited celebrities.

The Golden Gate wedding was the record company's idea. A publicity stunt to kick off the Match album and concert tour. At first Mom and Roger said no, but when the company offered to foot the bill and make all the arrangements they changed their minds.

I looked across the dance floor and spotted Angela. She was standing by the vegetable table munching on things that were good for her. She was a vegetarian like her dad. I guess I was too, now. "It's a much better way to eat," Mom had told me. She was probably right, but I missed hotdogs, cheese-burgers, chicken, beef, bologna sandwiches on white bread, and everything else I used to eat.

In the four months I'd known Angela we probably hadn't exchanged more than a thousand words. I'm thirteen, she's fifteen (but I'm taller). I like her, though she's always been quiet. Maybe she was shy. Or maybe she thought she was too old to hang out with her little brother-to-be. (But it turned out to be none of these things...not even close.) She was always standing or sitting off to the side—like she was now—watching everything, but rarely participating.

She has shoulder-length black hair with bangs, olive-colored skin, and dark brown eyes, which she usually covers with sunglasses. I look like my mom: curly straw-colored hair, green eyes, lanky. I thought I looked like a tall blond version of Harry Houdini (a stretch, I know) who had been my idol since I was about six years old.

Angela always carries a small, tattered, camouflage back-pack with her. She was carrying it now, slung over her shoulder. It didn't quite go with the long pink dress she was wearing. (And that was another thing about Angela. She didn't seem to care what she looked like, or what people thought of her.) In the pack was a book or two, a journal she was always scribbling in, sunglasses (several pairs), and by the bulk of it, a lot of other things I hadn't seen yet.

Cameras followed Mom and Roger's every move. Right now the newlyweds were in the middle of the dance floor. I snapped a couple of photos myself without anyone seeing, and then caught Angela's sunglasses watching me. I gave her a wave and headed in her direction. It was about time that I got to know my sister–whether she wanted to get to know me or not.

Brother & Sister

Angela was holding a plate of broccoli and carrots with a large glob of blue cheese dressing on the side.

"Some party," I said. "There must be three hundred people here."

"Two-hundred-fifty-six, I think," Angela said, surveying the crowd. "Counting guests, catering staff, reporters, and security people."

She couldn't have possibly known the exact number. People were bouncing around the arboretum like tennis balls. "How'd you know that?" I asked.

"By observing," she said with a slight smile.

I didn't know Angela well enough to know if she were kidding me or not. I looked over at the dance floor. Several other couples had joined Mom and Roger.

"I think this might be the first time we've actually been alone," I said. "Not that being with two-hundred-fifty-six people is being alone. But—"

"I know," Angela said. "Between your mom, my dad…"

She gestured toward the crowd. "...and everyone else, there's always someone around."

"I don't know about you," I said, "but I thought I was going to pass out if the ceremony went on a second longer."

"Me, too!" she said. "I felt woozy."

"Exactly!" This was about as friendly as Angela had ever been to me. Now that we were official stepbrother and sister maybe things had changed.

"What do you think caused that woozy feeling?" I asked.

"Stress maybe," Angela said.

"I guess I've never felt stress then," I said, "because I thought I was going to puke." This probably wasn't the right thing to say. Angela set her plate of vegetables and blue cheese dressing on the table. "Aside from the stress," I continued quickly, "what do you think of all of this?"

Angela shrugged. "I guess it all seems kind of orchestrated, as if—"

"We're on a reality TV show or something?" I said.

"In a way we are," Angela said. "They're going to incorporate the wedding into the music video." She looked at the crowd again and sighed. "I guess we'll have to get used to it."

"Nah..." I said. "It'll be fine once we get on the road. No one's going to follow us across the country to Philadelphia. You heard what they told Buddy."

"Speak of the devil." Angela pointed to a short, balding man bullying his way toward us through the crowd. He was flanked by two burly plainclothes security men running interference for him.

Buddy T.

Buddy T. is Mom and Roger's personal manager, or PM. No one knows what the T stands for, but Roger thinks it stands for To-Do, because when Buddy speaks it always sounds like he's reading a list.

Buddy is abrasive, arrogant, and supposedly one of the best PMs in the music business. His job is to deal with the booking agent and concert promoters, fill the venues with fans, and make sure the equipment, roadies, and musicians all show up on time ready to work and perform. It's an important and complicated job.

Mom and Roger don't get along with Buddy very well. He didn't want Angela and me to go on tour with them. Mom's response: "If they don't go, we don't go."

Buddy wanted to hire a driver to drive the tour bus. Roger's response: "For the next year the bus is our home. We're not staying in hotels. We don't want a stranger living in our home."

"Or driving our home," Mom added.

In between personal appearances, performances, recording sessions, and tour rehearsals Mom and Roger had squeezed in driving lessons so they could handle the bus safely.

Buddy asked for a detailed itinerary of our cross-country trip.

Roger's response: "We haven't decided what route we're taking to Philadelphia, where we're going to stop, or what detours we'll take. All you need to know is that we'll be at the Electric Factory in Philly in plenty of time for the first concert."

None of this had set well with Buddy. He had worked with some of the biggest names in the music business and was used to getting his way no matter how famous they were.

"One platinum song!" he had shouted during one of their meetings. "Big deal! Who do you two think you are? I don't have enough fingers and toes to count the number of one-hit wonders I've worked with in my life. One of them is a security guard now. Three of them sell insurance for a living. And they were all famous. I mean *really, really* famous…for a heartbeat or two. Now look at 'em."

What Buddy couldn't seem to grasp was that Roger and Mom had each sacrificed, or at least delayed, lucrative music careers to raise us.

"I've been on tour before," Mom told Buddy. "I got off the road because of Quest. I didn't want to raise him in that toxic atmosphere. Roger and I are going to do this tour our own way. We've taken them out of school for a year to see the United States and arranged for them to continue their schoolwork through the Internet. We're going to travel and act like the normal family we are. If we can't find a way to do this as a family we'll cancel the tour."

"Yeah?" Buddy said. "What about the record company? What about your contract?"

"If they dump us," Roger said, "so be it. I don't care if I'm playing in front of ten or ten thousand people. I'm not in this for the money or fame. I just want to write and play my music and I can do that in San Francisco just as well as I can do it on tour."

Buddy had laughed at this comment. "You'll change your *tune* once you get out on the road and feel those fans. If I could find a way to bottle and sell the high you're going to get on tour I'd be the richest man on earth."

Roger and Mom had gotten so fed up with Buddy they went to the record company to see what could be done to get rid of him. The president of the company was a woman named Heather Hughes who had known Mom for years and was a good friend. Long before Roger came into the picture she and Mom had jogged together three times a week. She was tall, blond, athletic, and very direct.

"I wouldn't get rid of Buddy if I were you," she advised. "Every band and solo artist hooked up with Buddy has come in here demanding the exact same thing. Here's what you need to know about Buddy. When you asked me for the name of a good PM, I didn't choose Buddy, he chose you. In the past two years I've begged him to manage a dozen different artists. He's turned me down flat every single time. He called *me* and asked for this job. He likes your music, and believe it or not, he likes you and your kids. I know he's a little rough around the edges, but when this is all over you're going to consider him a part of your family. Everyone else he's managed has. You will love him in the end."

That was hard for me to believe as I watched Buddy march up with a scowl on his face and grunt: "Time to go."

"What are you talking about?" I asked. "Mom and Roger are supposed to sing before we leave."

"They're going to sing," Buddy answered. "But you and Angela won't be here to hear it. They're doing a short set. A couple of songs, max, then they're outta here. I need you on the bus ready to go. It's a long trip from here to Philly."

"Why can't we just ride over to the bus with them after they finish?" Angela asked.

"Photo op," Buddy said. "The wedding's going to be part of their music video. It hits the air in a couple of days. You're not included in the video per your parents' request. Enough chitchat." He nodded at the two security men. "These two will drive you over."

The Bus

It was more like a rocket ship than a bus.

I sat down in the white leather driver's seat and stared at the rows of buttons and switches. I picked one and pushed it. A forty-two-inch plasma screen TV flipped open in front of the windshield.

"Whoa!" I swiveled the chair around and smiled at Angela.

"It's a lot nicer than I thought it would be," she said, running her hand along the back of one of the six leather chairs tucked under the polished rosewood dining table.

I jumped up from the driver's seat. "Let's check out the bedrooms!"

We walked to the back of the bus, passing a washer and dryer, stainless steel refrigerator, range, oven, microwave, dishwasher, a good-sized bathroom with a shower and tub, arriving at a rosewood pocket door that *swooshed* open with the push of yet another button. Behind the door was a huge bedroom with a closet (filled with clothes), a vanity, another plasma TV, a second bathroom, and *one* king-sized bed.

"This must be my bedroom," I said. "I wonder where you and the folks are going to sleep?"

Angela gave me a concerned smile.

"I'm sure our bedrooms are around here somewhere," I assured her.

"We can see *everywhere* from where we're standing," Angela said.

I didn't point out the fact that the bus was actually ten feet longer than the sailboat I was raised on. Instead, I stepped out of the bedroom, found a set of blue curtains along the wall across from the main bathroom, and pulled them open.

"Ta-da!" I said. "Bedrooms."

"Bunk beds," Angela corrected.

"On the boat we call them berths."

"They look more like coffins."

I hit two more buttons and lights came on above the beds. I flipped another switch and two small plasma TVs flipped down, one above each bed. "Coffins don't have reading lights or TVs," I pointed out. "And look..." I picked up the laptop computer on the lower bunk. "Dead people don't need computers."

There was an identical laptop on the top bunk. The computers would be our classroom for the next year.

"Do you want the top bunk or the bottom bunk?" I asked.

Angela spent a moment thinking about it. "Bottom, I guess."

"Let's take a look outside," I said.

"Why?" Angela asked.

"Storage," I said. "Mechanical stuff. The guts. Let's see what's stowed below deck and how this thing works."

The bus was parked in a parking lot on the other side of the Golden Gate Bridge off of highway 101 outside of San Rafael (Buddy's idea to trick the fans so we could get a "clean getaway" as he put it).

I started opening the compartments under the bus. The first two were filled with neatly arranged clear plastic storage containers. The containers were exactly the same size. Written on each in careful lettering was a detailed list of what was inside.

"Wow," I said. "Who did this?" I knew it wasn't Mom and I didn't think it was Roger's work either. He seemed pretty relaxed, except when it came to vegetables.

"It was me," Angela admitted. "I'm kind of an organization freak."

"I can see that," I said, wondering how she was going to get along with Mom who was the most disorganized human on earth. I closed the compartments, not sharing my concerns.

"It's really like a sailboat on wheels," I told Angela as I opened another compartment. "This is the generator. These are the house batteries. We don't have to be plugged into electricity for everything to work as long as the batteries are charged. I bet we could stay in this thing for a month without having to plug it in."

I opened the final compartment. "These are the holding tanks," I explained. "Gray water. Black water. Fresh water…"

"I know what fresh water is," Angela said. "Do I want to know what gray and black water are?"

"Probably not," I admitted. "But I'm going to tell you anyway. Gray water is water from the sinks and shower. Black water comes from the toilets."

"That's what I thought," Angela said. "Whose job is it to empty the tanks?"

"Your dad's," I said, hoping I was right.

Hooked to the back of the bus with a tow-bar was a brand new Range Rover, cherry red. Hanging on the back of the Rover were two mountain bikes, also red (the color no doubt picked by my mother, who had worn something red every single day of my life).

"Does your dad ride a bike?" I asked.

Angela shook her head. "How about your mom?"

"No way. They've either decided to take up biking, or the bikes are for us."

The Assignment

Back inside, I hit a few more buttons on the dash, then went over to the refrigerator to check out the contents, which looked nothing like the food on the sailboat.

Angela had retrieved her laptop and was sitting at the dining table booting up. She said something I didn't quite catch because I was wondering how a refrigerator could be completely full and still have nothing edible inside—at least anything I wanted to eat.

"What?" I asked.

"Maybe we should talk about our school assignment," Angela said.

I closed the refrigerator. "Now?"

She took off her sunglasses. "Why not?"

Angela was a straight-A student. So was I in the subjects I was interested in like math and writing. (I would have gotten As in Magic too if they taught it in school.)

"We'll have plenty of time later," I said. "It's not like we get to drive the bus. We'll just be sitting here watching the country pass by."

"It might be a good idea at least to get organized," Angela persisted. "We have to start working on this Web page. Figure out who's doing which part of the assignment."

I thought about the neatly stacked boxes in the storage compartments. This could be a very long year.

"What's the hurry?" I asked. "We just got here."

"Your mom told me you were a whiz in school," Angela said. "She said that your nickname was IQ."

Blabbermouth, I thought. I would have to talk to Mom about that.

"Do you want my theory on schoolwork?" Angela asked.

I didn't, but said, "Sure."

"If you get it out of the way, it leaves time for more interesting things," Angela said. "If you don't get it out of the way, then you feel distracted and a little guilty and the interesting things aren't nearly as interesting because you're worrying about what you should be doing rather than what you are doing."

I had wondered if and when she was going to pull the big sister thing on me. It hadn't taken long. "What do you mean by interesting things?" I asked.

"Things that you're really interested in besides schoolwork."

That was just about everything for me. "I'm going to change out of these clothes."

I pulled out a pair of baggy cargo pants from the drawer beneath the bunks and stepped into the bathroom. (I always wear cargoes because I have a lot of things to carry.)

I was thrilled about getting out of school for a year until I found out I wasn't really getting out of school for a year. I'd been transferred to Angela's school and was going to work with her teacher, Mr. Pallotta, even though Angela was two grades ahead of me. Mr. Pallotta was a nice guy, but a little too enthusiastic about the school thing for my taste. In addition to our regular schoolwork, Mr. Pallotta wanted us to put together a Web page of our tour. "It'll be fun!" he had said excitedly. But it sounded like a lot of extra work to me.

I came out of the bathroom and joined Angela at the table with a deck of cards (that's one of the things I carry in my pockets), which I started manipulating.

"Before we begin," I said. "I'd like to point out that school doesn't officially start until the day after tomorrow."

"We're not really starting," Angela said. "We're just planning how we're going to proceed. And what's with the cards?"

"Nervous hands," I said, cutting the deck with one hand. "That's what Mom calls it. I do my best thinking when my hands are busy."

"Well, this shouldn't take too much thinking," Angela said. "I don't know the exact route we're taking to Pennsylvania." She pulled up a map on her computer screen. "But I'm guessing we're passing through Nevada, Utah, Wyoming, Nebraska, Iowa, Illinois, Indiana, and Ohio before we get there. Nine states. Maybe more if we take side trips. I think we should include a few facts about each state even if we're just passing through it."

"I'll tell you right up front that I'm not very good at geography," I admitted. "Now, give me a math problem or a word puzzle. I can help you out with those."

"I guess the geography will be one of my responsibilities, then," Angela said. "We can create a map of our route as we go along, with facts about the different states, perhaps write a little bit about the places we stop, post photos, and maybe even upload video clips."

"I'll do the photos and video," I offered. Mom had given me a tiny digital camera for my birthday that did stills and video. I put the cards down and pulled the camera out of my pocket. "In fact I've already gotten started." I showed her some of the photos I'd taken at the wedding.

"Wait a second!" Angela said. She pointed to a photo of her eating broccoli. "I didn't see you take that of me."

"Yeah...well maybe I shouldn't have taken it so close-up."

"That's not the point," Angela said. "How did you take it without my knowing?"

"A lot of practice," I said. "I like candid photos. And I didn't have any choice at the wedding and the reception. Buddy made it clear that the only people allowed to take photos were the professional photographers hired by the record company."

"Okay, you're our official photographer," Angela said. "But I get veto power over what we use and what we don't use. Agreed?"

"Sure."

"Good. Now erase the one with me and the broccoli."

"Fine." I erased it. "What about the one of Buddy stomping

up to us with the security guards."

"No," Angela said, smiling. "I like that one." She closed her laptop.

"That's it?" I asked.

"It's a start," Angela said. She looked out the window for a moment then looked back at me. "One more thing."

I thought she was going to say something more about our assignment, but she had something very different on her mind.

"This all depends on us," she said quietly.

Mr. Pallotta told us that the Web page would count toward half our grades, which meant that Angela was depending on me for half of her grade. And Mom had made it clear that I was not to screw up Angela's grade point average.

"I'll do my part," I insisted.

"I'm not talking about the schoolwork now," Angela said. "I'm talking about the concert tour, the marriage…everything."

"You lost me," I said.

"This is a huge break for your mom and my dad," Angela said. "The album, the tour… Second chances like this don't come along very often. If we mess up they'll cancel the tour and lose their record contract."

She was right. There wouldn't be another big chance like this for my mom and her dad. They'd give it all up in a heartbeat if they thought the tour wasn't working out for me and Angela.

"So, we can't mess up," I said.

"We can't let them *know* when we mess up," Angela clarified, with a sly smile.

· · · · · ·

"It's not a bus," Buddy told me as soon as he barged in. "It's called a motor coach. You could buy ten *buses* for the price of this rig!"

Mom and Roger and the entourage didn't show up until midnight. Three encores held them up. There would have been a fourth, but according to Mom and Heather Hughes, Buddy literally pushed them off the stage.

"Wedding's over," Buddy had shouted into the microphone. "Go home." (Which I'm sure endeared him to everyone there).

Among the people wedged into the coach were Heather and my parents' agent (he books the concerts), their business manager (he handles the money), their lawyer (she negotiates the contracts), their producer (he makes the recordings), and their personal manager (that's Buddy)—he does everything else. That's the Match "team." And they all get paid by my parents. Some of them get a percentage of what my parents make. Others get an outright fee for their services. So, they all have a vested interest in how this tour goes—in other words, how much money the tour makes and how many albums it sells.

As everyone was ready to file out of the coach, Buddy gave the driver thing one last try.

"You sure you won't change your mind about a driver?" he shouted. "I can have one here in an hour."

Surprisingly, the entire team appeared to agree with Buddy, including Heather.

Some of their comments:

"With a driver you and Blaze could spend more time with your kids."

"Driving takes a lot out of you."

"You're not professional drivers and this thing is a beast."

"You could spend that time rehearsing, writing new material, fine-tuning your performance."

"We've already been over that," Mom said.

"A dozen times," Roger added. "Forget it, Buddy."

And with that we were off.

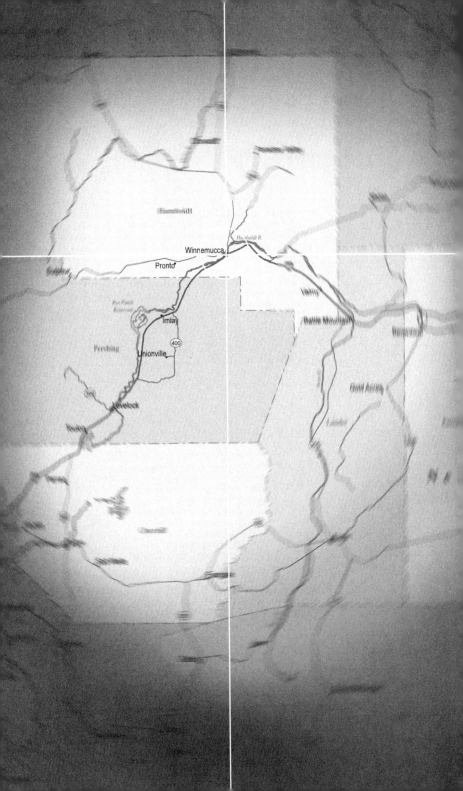

MONDAY, SEPTEMBER 1 >

Ziv took his right hand off the steering wheel and rubbed his dark eyes beneath his black-framed glasses.

"Do you want me to drive?" Eben asked.

"I'll be fine," Ziv answered. "I just need some coffee and maybe something to eat."

They had been driving for nearly four hours. Eben switched on the flashlight and looked at the map. "There's a town five miles ahead."

Ziv nodded.

Eben was glad he had not flown ahead with the others. The drive was giving him a chance to relax. As the miles went by, for the first time in what seemed like years, he was letting his guard down. And it felt good.

Ziv was an ideal traveling companion. He spoke only when necessary, leaving Eben ample time to think, which was exactly what he needed at that moment.

Along the edges of the headlights he watched the shadowy desert pass by mile after mile along the straight black road. It reminded him of trips he had taken with his younger brother, Aaron, through a similar landscape a world away. He would come home from a tough mission, pick up his brother, and take off with absolutely no destina-

tion in mind.

"Here's the town," Ziv said.

A single light burned straight ahead. The town was so small they might have missed it had they not been looking. They parked the blue SUV in front of a combination gas station, grocery store, and diner with a neon sign: Good Eats! Open 24 Hours 365 Days A Year including Christmas.

The coffee was strong and the breakfast was surprisingly good considering the desolate location and the time of morning.

Ziv sopped up the last of the egg yolk with his toast and popped it into his mouth. "Where are they now?" he asked.

Eben turned on his hand-held computer and enabled the tracking software. A highway map appeared on the small screen. "They're about fifty miles...wait a second." He zoomed in on the flashing icon. "It looks like they've stopped."

"Where?"

"On the side of the road," Eben said. "There's nothing around them."

The men got up, paid their bill, and hurried outside.

Ziv swore.

Their SUV was gone.

So much for letting myself relax, Eben thought angrily.

"What do you want to do?" Ziv asked.

Before Eben could answer, a state patrol cruiser pulled up in front of the diner with its lights flashing.

"I guess we report a stolen vehicle," Eben said. "Is your weapon on you?"

Ziv shook his head. "I left it in the SUV."

Eben had left his automatic pistol in the SUV too, which was just as well. American policemen were jumpy about people carrying guns.

Two state troopers got out of the car and slowly walked up to them.

"We're glad to see you," Eben said. "Someone has just stolen our car."

"How long ago was that?" one of the troopers asked. The nametag on his uniform shirt read: Williamson.

"It just happened," Eben said. "We were in the diner."

"Did you see them?" the other trooper asked. His last name was Arth.

"No, we were eating breakfast."

"Can I see some identification?" Williamson asked.

Eben looked at Ziv. "My papers were in the car."

"Mine too," Ziv said.

"Papers?" Arth said. "Where're you boys from?"

"Overseas," Eben said.

Williamson smiled. "Could you be more specific?"

"Israel," Eben said.

"Well, I guess you should come down to the station. You can file a stolen vehicle report there."

"Station?" Eben asked, looking around the tiny town.

"It's not here," Arth said. "We're about seventy miles back up the road."

"We don't have time for that," Eben said.

"You're going to have to make time," Williamson said.

"Are we under arrest?"

"No, but if you like we can arrange that. Besides, there are no car rental places around here. Think about it as a free ride."

"On one condition," Arth added.

"What's that?" Eben asked.

"We're going to have to frisk you before you get into the back of the cruiser. Standard operating procedure." Williamson gave them a quick frisk. "What's this?" He pulled the hand-held computer out of Eben's back pocket.

"It's a computer," Eben answered.

"Never seen one this small. I didn't know they have wireless in the diner."

"They don't," Eben said.

"We'll just hang onto it," Williamson said.

"Suit yourself." Eben wasn't worried. The files were all encrypted.

Eben and Ziv got into the backseat.

"How did you happen to arrive at the diner at the very moment our vehicle was stolen?" Eben asked.

"Got a call from someone," Arth said. "He suggested we pick you up and make sure you weren't terrorists."

Eben gave a harsh laugh. "We're the exact opposite of terrorists."

"We'll see about that," Williamson said.

Arth peeled out of the lot and tore down the highway with the siren blaring.

"So much for relaxing," Eben muttered.

"What?" Ziv asked.

"Never mind," Eben said with a sigh.

Boone & Crockett

I was up and out of my berth at 6 A.M.

I probably would have slept a lot longer if my stomach hadn't growled me awake. The coach was parked. Mom or Roger must have pulled into an RV park to get a little shut-eye. Angela was still asleep too.

I dumped a load of bran cereal into a bowl and soaked it with nonfat organic milk. I decided to take my feast outside so I wouldn't wake anyone with the alarming gurgling noises coming from my stomach. If I were lucky maybe the RV park would have a little store or a vending machine with candy bars or crackers.

No such luck.

Roger and Mom had not pulled into an RV park in the middle of the night. They had pulled off onto the shoulder of the straightest road I had ever seen. No buildings, no trees. In fact, there wasn't anything higher than my knees in any direction for as far as I could see.

Nevada, I thought. Has to be.

I stepped outside and closed the door.

And that's when the dog snuck up behind me and barked. I'm not sure what flew higher, me or the bowl of bran. But when I came down the cereal was all over me and the dog was nibbling flakes from the sand near my bare feet.

The dog had a broad flat head, pointed ears, a cropped tail, dusty gray fur, one brown eye, and one really weird blue eye that looked like it could see right through me. When the dog finished snapping up the last pitiful flake he looked up at me and gave me a doggy grin. He was missing several teeth. I saw he had a tag dangling from his collar. I bent down to see who he was and where he was from...

"Mornin'."

I snapped back up.

Standing in front of me was an old man with a long gray beard and matching hair braided halfway down his back. He had pale eyes, either light blue or gray (It was hard to tell in the early morning light.) He was thin, tan, and wrinkled (like a desert tortoise that had misplaced its shell).

"Hope Croc didn't startle you," the man said with a slight southern drawl.

"No," I lied, then squatted down and patted Croc's head to make it look good. "Croc, huh?" I said. "Doesn't seem like he'd eat you."

"Short for Crockett, not the reptile."

I looked up and down the road expecting to see a car or truck parked nearby, but there was no sign of one.

"Where'd you come from?" I asked.

"The name's Boone," he said sticking his hand out, ignoring my question.

I gave him a milky handshake. "Q," I said.

"Like in cue ball?"

"No, like in the letter Q."

He grinned. "Short for Quinn, Quentin, Quartermaster–"

"Quartermaster?" I said.

"A character in the James Bond novels," Boone said. "Also known as Q."

"My real name is Quest," I said, knowing he would never guess it. My dad named me. (When I got older Mom offered to have my name legally changed, but by then I had gotten used to it.)

Boone looked at the coach for a second or two then said, "Kind of an odd place to park a seven-hundred-fifty-thousand-dollar rig."

"Seven-hundred-fifty-thousand dollars?" I thought Buddy had been exaggerating.

"Could be worth more," Boone said. "Depends on how tricked out it is inside."

Maybe it was because I hadn't gotten much sleep, or maybe it was because I was starving. But it wasn't until that moment that an alarm went off in my head. What were Boone and Croc doing out in the middle of nowhere at the crack of dawn with no visible means of transportation except their six legs?

Boone must have either heard the alarm in my head or saw the alarm in my face. "Problem?" he asked.

"You mean with the...uh...rig?"

"Yeah."

I shrugged. "Not that I know of."

Boone got down on his back and wiggled underneath the coach until just his scuffed cowboy boots stuck out. Croc walked over to my cereal bowl and started licking it.

"My pack's around back," Boone said. "Go fetch it."

"What are you doing?" I asked.

"Fixin' your rig."

What was I going to do? Grab him by his cowboy boots and yank him out from under the coach? A burglar doesn't usually offer to fix your house before he robs it. I went around back and found the pack leaning against the Rover. Next to it was a smaller daypack, a sleeping bag rolled out on the gravel shoulder, a little propane stove, a James Bond 007 novel (I guess that's where he came up with Quartermaster), and a mug of coffee steaming in the cool desert air.

I hefted the big backpack—which had to weigh at least seventy-five pounds—onto my shoulder and lugged it around the side of the coach.

Boone's cowboy boots were still sticking out from under the coach. Croc was lying down with the empty bowl between his front paws, looking disappointed.

"Why don't you go out and catch a rabbit?" I suggested. "We'll split it."

"What?" Boone asked.

"Nothing." I set the backpack down.

"There's a toolkit in the front pocket," Boone said.

I found the kit and pulled it out, but hesitated before sliding it under the coach. "Maybe I should get my mom or Rog... uh...my dad."

"Unless they're mechanics," Boone said, "they ain't gonna be much help. Your folks didn't pull over because they were tired. They broke down."

"Can you fix it?"

"Not unless you slide me them tools."

I was saved from making a decision by the coach door opening. Mom stepped out first, followed by Roger, then Angela–all of them looking as if they had been awake about four seconds.

"What's going on out here?" Mom asked.

"What time is it?" Roger asked.

"Where are we?" Angela asked.

I answered their questions in order. "There's a guy trying to fix the coach. 6:20. I think we're in Nevada."

Boone slid out from underneath the coach, looked up at the sleepy newcomers, and grinned.

"Mornin' Blaze," he said.

Winnemucca

The coach *had* broken down during the night and rather than wake us, Roger and Mom decided to pull off the road and figure out what to do after they got some sleep.

Boone managed to fix the problem with a paper clip and a strip of duct tape. "Should be enough to get the rig to a garage in Winnemucca," he said. "But you're gonna have to baby the rig along or it'll bust again."

Mom asked Boone if he would do the "babying" and he cheerfully agreed to drive.

A couple of hours later we were sitting in a café across the street from a garage in Winnemucca, Nevada. We had invited Boone to breakfast, but he passed. He wanted to keep an eye on the mechanic and make sure he fixed the problem correctly.

"Who is this Boone guy?" Roger asked.

"He might be the oldest roadie on earth," Mom answered. "His name is Tyrone Boone, but everyone calls him Boone. I haven't seen him since Q was born. He's been touring with bands off and on since the seventies. He toured with my old band for eight months."

"What does he play?" Angela asked as the waitress set plates of fruit in front of her and Roger.

Mom jumped in before I could answer. "He's not a musician," she explained. "A roadie is someone who sets up equipment before a show, breaks it down afterward, then hauls it to the next gig. It's hard work with no glory and it doesn't pay much. Most roadies do it for two or three years for the adventure then find real jobs."

"Boone's been doing this for thirty years?" I asked. "How old is he?"

"I'm not sure he's still a roadie," Mom answered. "And I'm not sure how old he is." She looked out the front door where Croc was lying. "It's odd because Boone doesn't look like he's aged a day in thirteen years, and what's even stranger is that he had a dog just like Croc when he toured with us. Same name, same age, same missing teeth, same weird blue eye."

"That can't be the same dog," Roger said, following her gaze.

"Of course not," Mom said. "But I swear he looks exactly like the old Croc."

"What did Boone say to you, Q?" Roger asked.

I was mesmerized for a moment by a waitress walking by with a platter of sizzling bacon, fried eggs, and crisp hash browns.

"Q?" Mom said.

"Oh...uh...not much." I picked up my spoon and scooped up a glob of blue yogurt the same color as the toothpaste I'd brushed my teeth with that morning. "He crawled underneath the coach and asked me to get his tools."

"It doesn't make sense," Roger said. "Our name isn't on our coach. Why would he fix our coach without finding out who we were first?"

Mom picked at a chunk of watermelon with her fork. "There aren't too many coaches like ours on the road," she said. "And most of them are hauling around musicians."

"I still don't get it," Roger said.

"Boone has been around for a long time," Mom continued. "If there were musicians inside, even if he didn't know them, they would probably know him—at least by reputation. He's kind of a legend. The guy can fix anything. When he was touring with us he was always being flown off in private jets to fix shows that were having technical problems. At least that's what he said."

"What do you mean?" Angela asked.

"Oh nothing," Mom said. "There are always wild rumors flying around on tours. Some of the roadies thought he worked for the government, and some thought he was on the run." Mom laughed. "There were even some who thought he was a spy."

"You're kidding?" I said.

"Just crazy rumors," Mom said, smiling. "He is a little odd though. Whenever he flew off to fix a show he'd always come back by car, bus, or train, never by airplane. Boone is terrified of flying."

"I didn't see any railway tracks where we broke down," Roger pointed out. "And it sure wasn't a bus stop. How did he arrive outside our coach in the middle of the night, in the middle of nowhere?"

They all looked at me. I shrugged. "He was just there when I stepped outside. He had his sleeping bag rolled out behind the rig with a spy novel sitting next to it."

"James Bond?" Mom asked.

"Yeah. How'd you know?"

"Because he got all of us hooked on Ian Fleming's 007 novels when he was on tour with us. That's probably where the spy rumor got started." Mom smiled. "*On Her Majesty's Secret Service, License to Kill...* I couldn't get enough of..."

She looked at Roger and her smiled faded. Roger had a rather sour look on his face. Angela also looked uncomfortable. It seemed like a strange reaction to some old spy novels.

"What's the..." I started, but Mom cut me off with one of her *looks.*

"It was years ago," she said. "Boone's a good guy."

"I guess we should be grateful he showed up when he did regardless of how he got there," Roger said, recovering from whatever had bothered him.

At that moment Tyrone Boone came into the café and walked over to our table. Croc remained outside, staring through the window, drooling. I wondered if they had doggie bags for yogurt.

"The mechanic knows what he's doin'," Boone said. "Should have you back on the road in under an hour."

"We really appreciate your help, Boone," Roger said. "Now why don't you join us and have some breakfast?"

"Appreciate the offer," Boone said. "But I need to get

goin'."

"Where *are* you going?" Mom asked.

Boone shrugged.

"Are you still doing the roadie thing?"

"Off and on," he said. "By the way. I caught your new album." He gave Mom and Roger an admiring grin. "It's outstanding. Not a bad track on it. I think Match is going to have a good run."

"Thanks," Roger said. "You saved us out there on the road. I feel like we should pay you, or—"

"Forget it," Boone said.

"How did you end up in the middle of the desert?" Mom asked.

Boone looked a little sheepish and glanced away.

"What's going on, Boone?" she asked suspiciously.

After a pause, Boone said, "Buddy T."

Roger laughed. "I should have guessed."

"I'm real sorry," Boone said. "He had me lined up to be your driver if he could talk you into takin' one on. Guess he couldn't get you to agree, which was fine with me. I don't blame you for wantin' to spend time with your kids on your own."

"So, what happened?" Mom asked.

"He called me up last night and told me he'd hired some kid to follow you across the country. You know, just to make sure things were okay. He asked me to ride along. 'Just in case,' as he put it—thinkin' that somewhere down the road you might have a problem and take me on to help since we knew each other."

"That guy just doesn't give up!" Roger said.

"I didn't feel right about doggin' you," Boone continued, looking a little hangdog himself. "But you know how it is. I couldn't afford to turn Buddy down. This is a small business and Buddy has a lot of clout. Getting hooked up with a tour has been hard for me the past few years. They're lookin' for young studs that can jack around heavy amps, lights, and stage props.

"Anyway, we were about a half hour behind you when you broke down. When we caught up, all the lights were out, so I thought I'd just hang out 'til morning to see if you needed help."

"What about the kid?" Roger asked.

"I sent him back last night. I told him that if Buddy called he should tell him we lost you. The kid was happy to go. He's a young guitar player who Buddy's trying to give a leg up in the biz. He was happy to get back to his gal in San Fran."

"Now what are you going to do?"

"I'll go over and make sure everything's okay with the coach. There are a lot of components on those things, but you shouldn't have any more problems. Then I'll hitch a ride back to the city." He gave us a shy grin. "No hard feelin's?"

"Not from us," Mom said. "But Buddy's not going to be happy with you or the guitar player."

Boone shrugged. "Buddy's never happy, but don't be too hard on him. He's just doing his job and he takes it seriously."

"A little too seriously," Roger said, then added, "You've obviously had a lot of experience driving these coaches."

"Couple million miles."

"Will you do me another favor?"

"Sure thing."

"Don't take off until we get over there. We've been checked out on everything, but I still have some questions. Do you think you can stick around to answer a few more?"

"No problem."

Boone walked out of the café. Croc continued to stare at us through the window.

"What will happen to him?" Roger asked Mom.

"I suspect that Buddy promised him a position on our tour if he managed to hook up with us and get us to Philly," she said. "I guess he'll head back to San Francisco and see if he can hire on with another tour."

"What are the chances of that happening?" Roger asked.

"He might get some short gigs with small bands, but nothing long-term without Buddy putting in a good word for him."

"That's what I thought." Roger looked at me and Angela. "What do you two think of taking on another passenger?"

"I like him," I said.

"I do too," Angela added.

Roger sighed. "What about that pit bull of his?"

"It's not a pit bull," Angela said. "Boone told me Croc was a cross between a Blue Heeler and a Border Collie."

"Did he happen to tell you how old Croc was?" I asked.

"I didn't ask," Angela said.

I'd always wanted a dog, but I had a pup in mind, not a great-great-grandcanine.

Roger looked out at Croc. "Do you think Boone will *let* us give him a bath?"

I looked over at the ancient dog and wondered if Croc would let us give him a bath.

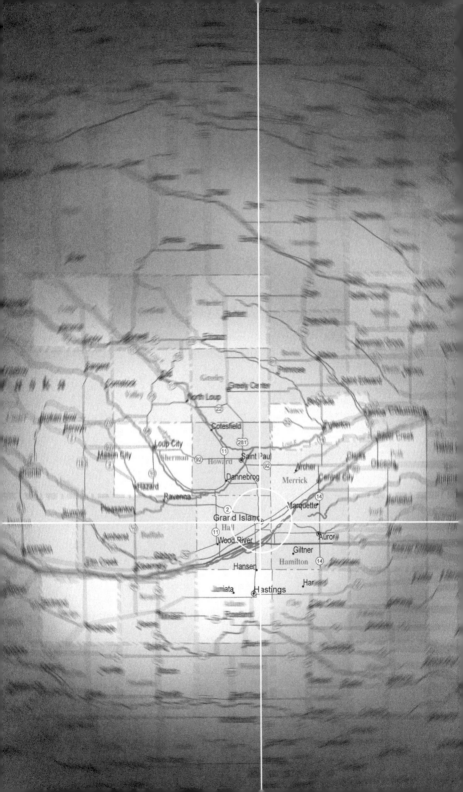

WEDNESDAY, SEPTEMBER 3 >

East

Croc did not like his bath, but he tolerated it as long as Angela and I slipped him bits of buttered toast as a reward for not biting us. We used the hose in back of the mechanic's shop to do the job. After we finished Croc didn't look much better, but at least he was reasonably clean.

Aside from being an expert driver and mechanic, Boone was a walking (or driving) USA encyclopedia. We didn't pass a single town he hadn't been to before. Not only that, he appeared to know everything about these towns going back a hundred years or more. As we drove he would give us geographical and historical tidbits for our Web page assignment.

When we passed through Cheyenne, Wyoming, he said, "If your parents' band was on tour in the 1860s they'd be travelin' in a private Union Pacific Railroad coach called a Pullman—not a coach like this. Every act from New York stopped in Cheyenne to perform on their way to San Francisco. There were several small theaters in town and a good-sized opera house. You ever heard of Lillie Langtry?"

We hadn't.

"Lillie Langtry played in Cheyenne. She was the musical diva of her day. No one knew what Lillie would do next, but whatever it was, she did it in a big way and made sure everybody knew about it."

"How do you know all this stuff?" I asked.

"Books," he said. "Everything you need to know can be found in a book."

We didn't write about Lillie Langtry specifically, but we did something for the Web page comparing how musicians made their living in the 1860s to how it works now.

During the day we drove east on Interstate 80, stopping in small towns and tourist attractions in Utah, Wyoming, and Nebraska. At night we pulled into RV parks, hooked up the coach, and ate dinner—usually cooked by Roger. There was nothing wrong with the food, or Roger's cooking—some of it even tasted good. But what I couldn't figure out was how I could eat an entire plate heaped with food and afterward feel as if I hadn't eaten anything at all.

Roger and Mom hadn't driven an hour since Boone joined us. They gave him a compartment to store his stuff and offered to let him sleep on the sofa bed inside, but he preferred to sleep outside with Croc. I joined them one of the nights, hoping Boone might have some meat stashed in that big backpack of his. He didn't. He appeared to live on bottled water and air.

About three quarters of the way across Nebraska I thought I would starve to death before we reached Philly.

I was sitting next to Boone in the passenger seat, practicing some rope tricks (which I'm pretty good at) when Boone pointed out a sign for a town called Grand Island. He turned to Mom and Roger who were working on a new song. "If I remember right," Boone said. "There's a decent farmer's market in Grand Island. Good place to replenish our veggie supplies and stretch our legs."

Grand Island was not an island and it wasn't exactly grand, but it turned out to be a great place to stretch our legs, or in my case my shrunken belly.

I usually stuck with Boone and Croc while Roger, Mom, and Angela explored vegetable opportunities.

Boone was dead serious about books and a lot smarter than he sounded. When he wasn't driving he was reading, and not just spy novels. History, current affairs, philosophy, poetry, classics, self-help books, science...there didn't seem to be a subject he wasn't interested in, or a subject he didn't know something about. His storage compartment under the coach was beginning to look like a small public library. He seemed to have a sixth sense about where to locate the biggest used bookstore in any given town. It was as if he could smell a collection of mildewed books. And Grand Island was no exception.

I followed Boone's nose to a used bookstore about half a block from the market.

"Are you interested in thrillers and spy novels?" Boone asked as we entered the dim store with more books than there were shelves to hold them.

"I'm not sure," I said.

"Well, this is a Spy-Fi goldmine!" Boone pointed to the

shelves. "John le Carré, Len Deighton, Graham Greene, Helen MacInnes, Ken Follett, Eric Ambler, Robert Ludlum…"

I hadn't heard of any of these authors.

He slipped his daypack off his shoulder, picked up a stack of paperbacks, and wiped the dust off the covers. "Look at these. Three pristine Ian Flemings with original cover illustrations! *Goldfinger, The Man with the Golden Gun,* and *Dr. No.* There's nothin' like a good 007 yarn, although they aren't exactly politically correct. He wrote them in the '50s and we had different outlooks back then."

"I've seen some of the James Bond movies," I said.

"Then you don't know anything about James Bond," Boone scoffed. He held up *Dr. No.* "You gotta read this. Did you know that Lee Harvey Oswald was reading *Dr. No* the night before he assassinated President Kennedy in 1963?"

I shook my head.

"But here's the weird thing," Boone continued. "That same night, JFK was reading the same book in his hotel room."

That was weird, but I still wasn't sure I was interested in reading James Bond.

I watched Boone sort through some more books, then I glanced out the window thinking I might wander over to the market. What I saw across the street wiped that idea from my brain. It wasn't Goldfinger or a man with a golden gun. It was a golden arch. I started salivating.

"You're gonna love these gems," Boone said, holding up two more paperbacks.

Not as much as I'm going to love the two cheeseburgers and an order of fries, I thought.

"I'm going across the street to use the restroom," I said.

Boone nodded distractedly and headed down another dark aisle in search of more gems.

Ziv dropped Eben at the Salt Lake City airport.

By the time they got untangled from the state police they were out of tracking range and knew they would never catch up. Eben decided to fly ahead and leave Ziv to drive the SUV, which the state troopers had miraculously found twelve hours after it had been stolen, one mile from the diner. The only damage was to the ignition where the thief had hotwired the SUV to get it started.

"Anything missing?" Arth asked.

"No," Eben lied. His automatic and Ziv's were both gone. They were not going to be easy to replace.

"Lucky," Arth said.

"Weird," Williamson said.

The troopers had checked their passports and visas, made a phone call—presumably to the person who had tipped them off—then sent them on their way.

It was obvious that someone had been following them. But who? Eben wondered. And were they still watching?

Food for Thought

I crossed the street with Croc at my heels, looking both ways, making sure the veggie patrol didn't see me slip beneath the Golden Arches.

"Two cheeseburgers, fries, and a chocolate shake," I said, then looked at Croc staring gluttonously at me through the window. "Make that three cheeseburgers."

"For here or to go?"

"For here."

"Would you like that supersized?'

"Absolutely."

The order was up within a minute. I took my food around the corner where I couldn't be seen from the street and almost dropped my tray when I saw who was sitting in the very last booth next to the wall.

"Mind if I join you?" I asked.

Angela nearly choked on her Big Mac and her face turned as pink as the strawberry shake in front of her.

I laughed and sat down across from her. "You're about

the last person in the world I thought I'd see in here," I said. I unwrapped my first cheeseburger and added, "With the exception of your dad of course."

"Are you going to tell?" Angela asked.

"Nope." I popped a salty fry into my mouth, thinking that my new sister and I were going to get along after all.

Angela gave me a grateful smile. "I guess there are some things we don't know about each other."

"Yeah," I said. "Like just about everything." I took a huge satisfying bite out of my cheeseburger. "I don't suppose your dad ever sneaks into a place like this for something to eat."

Angela shook her head. "Never, but my mom..." She bit her lower lip and looked away.

I looked away too. Angela's mom had died four years earlier.

Angela looked back at me. "Anyway," she continued. "My dad is a true vegetarian. And I agree with the practice at least in theory. But it's hard to stick with the diet when your friends are eating stuff like this."

"Yeah," I said. "Also because stuff like this tastes good." I finished off my first cheeseburger in three bites and began unwrapping the second. "Do you have any other big secrets I should know about?"

"Yes," Angela admitted. "But I think it's only fair that you tell me one of your secrets before I give you another one of mine," she said.

"You didn't exactly offer up your burger secret voluntarily, but I guess I could give you something. But before I do, define 'secret' for me."

"What do you mean?"

"If I tell you something is it just between you and me, no one else, including your dad, my mom, or any other human being?" I held up my right hand after licking some ketchup off of it. "So help you God?"

Angela held up her right hand. "I swear."

"Okay," I said. "But I still don't understand why you don't tell your dad about this." I pointed to the food on the table. "I don't know him very well, but he seems pretty laid back."

"He is. And I don't think he would mind me eating a burger once in awhile, but it's complicated. I guess I don't want to disappoint him. Besides, staying away from this kind of food is better for you."

"If you can," I said. "I think my mom's going along with the vegetarian thing in order to lose some weight."

"Your mom looks great," Angela said.

"I think so too," I said. "But she's gotten more self-conscious about her looks since the album came out."

"So has my dad," Angela said. "The old Roger Tucker wore sweatpants, sandals, T-shirts, and rarely shaved more than once a week. Now he shaves every day—even in the coach. He's bought a whole new wardrobe and goes to a hair stylist. He used to cut his own hair, believe it or not."

"It's all part of the job," I said. "My real dad wears ripped jeans, torn shirts, ratty-looking sneakers, but he pays a fortune for them at the best boutiques in L.A. I guess you don't care about your image until other people start caring about your image."

"What about that secret?" Angela persisted.

"It will cost you two fries," I said.

"All right."

I took two of her fries and put one of them on my right palm and one on my left, then closed my hands over them.

"What are you doing?" Angela asked.

"Take off your sunglasses."

She pushed them to the top of her head.

"When I grow up," I said. "I want to become a magician."

"That's not too surprising," Angela said. "Considering both your mother and father are musicians."

Angela misheard me—a common mistake considering my parents' profession. My dad is a famous lead guitarist named Peter Paulsen, but he's better known by the nickname "Speed," which is also the name of his band, which Mom used to sing with. I don't see him much, which is just as well, because he is kind of crazy. I had no desire to play guitar, or sing like my mother—even if I could.

"*Magician*," I said. "Not musician."

"Like in magic?" Angela asked.

I opened my hands. The French fries were gone.

Angela reached across the table and turned my hands over. There were no fries hidden under them. "How did you do that?"

"Magic," I said.

"That's why you're always playing with the cards and ropes."

"That and my nervous hands," I said. "Your turn now. What do you want to become when you grow up?"

Angela bit her lower lip.

"Well?" I said.

Her answer was interrupted by two police cars roaring passed McDonald's with their sirens blaring. We jumped up and ran outside to see what was happening and almost collided with Boone and Croc. I unwrapped the cheeseburger and gave it to Croc, which he swallowed in two gulps.

Boone was holding a shopping bag filled with paperbacks, staring up the street in the direction the police cars had gone. A huge crowd of people was gathered at the edge of the farmer's market half a block away.

"Has there been an accident?" Angela asked.

"That's no accident," Boone said, pointing at the crowd. "I wondered how long it would take to catch up to us."

"What are you talking about?" I asked.

"Fame," Boone answered.

Fame

Boone was right.

By the time we reached the farmer's market the crowd had nearly doubled in size. At the center of the swarm were Mom and Roger (both looking a little dazed) smiling for the camera phones and signing scraps of paper and CDs.

Angela and I started to wiggle into the crowd to get closer, but Boone stopped us. "Better hang back here with me," he said.

"Why?" I asked.

"Your folks are fine," Boone answered. "And I think they want you to stay off the radar. Believe me, it's better if you do."

I jumped up to get a better view and snap a couple of photos for myself. The police had made it to the center of the crowd and were flanking Mom and Roger.

"How did this happen?" Angela asked. "We've been traveling for three days, stopped half a dozen times, and no one's paid any attention to us."

"The publicity machine is in motion," Boone told us. "Buddy and the record company have been busy. I suspect

that your parents have been plastered all over those TV enter-
tainment shows the past couple of days. Their wedding, pre-
views of the *Rekindled* video, interviews... Have they had their
cell phones on?"

"I don't know," I said.

"I haven't heard a call come in since I joined up with
you," Boone said. "I'm sure it wasn't their intention, but nothing fuels the publicity machine better than lack of contact.
Absence makes the heart grow fonder. They—"

"Are these the kids?"

We turned around and were assaulted by a barrage of
bright flashes. The man holding the expensive-looking camera was short, unshaven, and rumpled.

"Angie and Quest, right?" he said as he continued to take
pictures. "Angie, take off those shades so I can see those beautiful eyes."

Angela left her shades exactly where they were. "My name
is Angela," she said.

"And my name is Q," I added.

"Stop," Boone said, holding his hand over the camera lens.

"Hey, Boone. Didn't see you standing there. You their
babysitter or something?"

"I'm their friend," Boone said. "And if you don't stop, the
next photo you take will be of the inside of your colon."

"Just doing my job," the man said.

Croc trotted forward, fixed his weird blue eye on the man
and began moving toward him, growling.

"Okay, okay, Boone," the man said, backing away from
Croc. "I'll stop."

"You know each other?" Angela asked.

"Unfortunately," Boone said. "This is Dirk Peski, also known as the Paparazzi Prince."

Dirk gave us a theatrical bow and a grin.

"Is this your doin'?" Boone asked, gesturing toward the crowd.

"Not directly," Dirk said. "All I did was snap some pics of them buying a bunch of bananas. That's all it took. A couple of kids recognized them and asked for autographs. Then someone got on their cell, and the person they called got on their cell… You know how it goes. Big news in Grand Island."

"How'd you find us?" Boone asked.

"Wasn't easy, but I figured you'd be traveling Interstate 80. I flew into Salt Lake a few days ago, rented a car, and started trolling with my CB. A trucker spotted your coach and saw you take the exit up here."

"What are you going to do with the photos?" I asked.

"I'll upload them onto the Internet, send them out on the wire services. Your faces will be all over the world in about fifteen minutes. You'll be famous!"

This is exactly what Mom and Roger didn't want. I wondered how the Paparazzi Prince would like it if I uploaded the eight photos I had just secretly taken of him taking photos of us?

"How about leavin' the kids out of it," Boone said.

"How about arranging an exclusive interview with the rock stars and I'll think about it?" Dirk answered.

· · · · · ·

Mom and Roger weren't happy about Dirk's deal, but they agreed to the interview in order to keep Angela and me out of the news. It worked, but nothing was the same after Grand Island.

Boone guessed right. Mom and Roger had their cell phones off. They turned them on after we dumped Dirk and pulled back onto Interstate 80. Between them there were over fifty messages, mostly from Buddy. Mom put her phone on speaker. Each of Buddy's messages was louder than the previous message. His main points:

1. Their album, *Rekindled*, had hit #1 on Billboard.
2. The concert tour was sold out and he was booking extra concert dates.
3. Mom and Roger had dozens of appearance offers including three network morning shows.
4. Why don't you return my calls!
5. Turn on your cell phones!
6. Who do you think you are!

Mom expected the album to do well, but not that well, and not that quickly. Roger asked Boone how long it would take to get to Philadelphia. Boone thought he could get there in less than twenty-four hours if Roger and Mom helped with the driving.

That didn't work out. Mom and Roger were too busy talking on their cell phones to drive. Friends calling with congratulations, TV, radio, and newspaper reporters wanting interviews, and of course Buddy with new developments, questions, and demands.

I worried that the sudden attention they got in Grand Island might make Roger nervous or change his mind about the tour. But just the opposite happened. He was completely stoked. Mom was a little calmer about it, but she was used to the attention. The band she'd been in with Dad was famous.

After a few miles I put down my deck of cards and pulled out one of the 007 books Boone had been raving about. He was right. The book was a lot better than the movie.

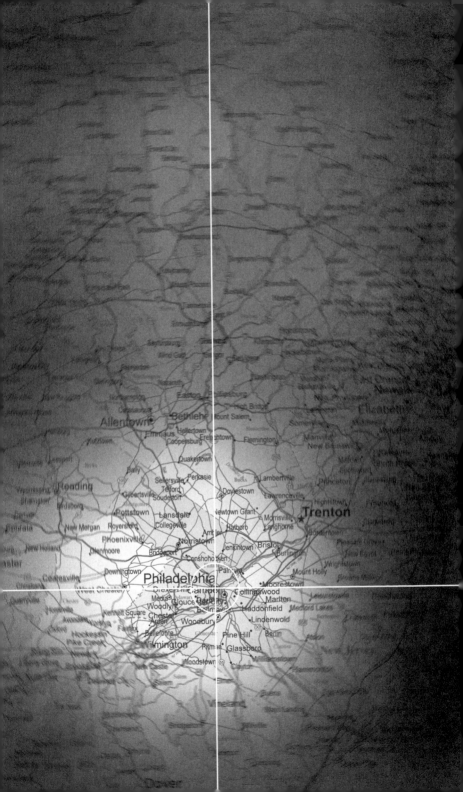

THURSDAY, SEPTEMBER 4 >

Secret Service

I was still reading at one o'clock in the morning when I heard Angela outside my curtain.

"Are you awake?" she whispered.

Reluctantly, I closed *007* and parted the curtains. Angela was holding a McDonald's cheeseburger.

"You and I are going to get along great," I said, climbing down. "Where did you get that?"

"Truck stop," Angela answered. "Boone just filled up with diesel."

"I was so busy reading *Dr. No* I didn't even know we stopped."

"That's my favorite Ian Fleming," Angela said.

"You've read them?"

"All thirteen."

I wondered why she hadn't mentioned this when the subject came up in Winnemucca.

"What did you think of the centipede scene?" Angela asked. "It still gives me the creeps when I think about it."

"The giant squid and crawling through the tarantulas was just as bad." I climbed down from my berth and glanced at the bedroom door. It was closed. "Are they asleep?"

Angela nodded. I followed her and the burger into the kitchen. Boone was at the wheel speeding down the dark freeway listening to a radio talk show about UFOs. Croc was curled up on the leather passenger seat. We sat down at the table.

"Did you already eat?" I asked, taking the cheeseburger.

"I wasn't hungry," Angela said.

"You sure you don't want half?"

"I'm fine."

I was glad to hear it. I unwrapped the burger, took a bite then asked her why she was up so late.

Angela shrugged. "I guess I'm just excited about all the things that happened yesterday."

"It's just the beginning," I said. "Grand Island isn't exactly the center of the music universe. Wait until we get to Philly."

"Are you happy for them?" Angela asked.

"Sure. Like you said, second chances like this don't happen very often. Match is on its way." I finished the last of the cheeseburger, wishing she had gotten a bag full. "How do you feel about it?"

"I'm happy for them too," Angela answered. "But I didn't realize how much time it takes to be famous. They were on their phones for hours and would still be talking if they hadn't turned the phones off and gone to sleep."

I nodded. "Most of Mom's friends are famous musicians, and believe me, they work hard to stay famous. And there's

no such thing as bad press. Anytime they make the news...
good or bad...musicians make money. They complain about
people like Dirk Peski, but there's a parasitic relationship
between paparazzi and pop stars."

"That's a lot of Ps," Angela said, grinning. "Is that why
you want to become a magician instead of a musician?"

"Real funny," I said. "And for your information, magicians
work just as hard as musicians. You can't believe how much
practice it takes." I wadded up the burger wrapper, closed it
in my hand then made it disappear.

Angela laughed. "You have to show me how you do that.
And practice is another P."

"Yeah?" I said. "Here's another P... Check your right
pocket."

"What are you talking about?" Angela asked, reaching
into her bathrobe pocket.

"No way!" She held up a yellow burger wrapper folded
into an origami crane. "How−"

I shook my head. "Before the minor riot in Grand Island
you were going to tell me what you wanted to be when you
grow up."

"I hadn't decided if I was going to tell you or not," Angela
said, biting her lower lip.

One of the skills a good magician has is the ability to read
people. Angela wanted to spill her guts.

"But you have now," I said.

"How do you know that?"

"Because when you want to say something, but you're not
sure you want to say it, you bite your lower lip."

"I do not!"

"Every time," I said. "Here's another P. In poker it's called a *tell*. Magicians use it to read their audience. Just spit it out."

Angela paused then said, "Do you know anything about my mom?"

I hadn't expected this. My mom had warned me not to bring up Angela's mother. "It's a raw subject for Angela," she had said. "Don't go there."

"You don't have to talk about this if you don't want to," I said.

"I want to," Angela said. "Do you know what happened to her?"

The burger in my stomach started to churn. "Mom said she died for her country."

Angela nodded. "Do you know what she did for a living?"

"I figured she was in the military over in Iraq or Afghanistan," I said. "Mom was kind of vague about the details."

"My mother was a Secret Service agent," Angela said.

It looked like Mom had been more than vague. "Like in protecting the president of the United States Secret Service?" I asked.

"More Ps," Angela answered, but her smile was gone. "That's only a small part of what the Secret Service does. When I was five years old she was on presidential detail for six months. We moved to D.C. to be close to her, but we might as well have stayed in San Francisco. Dad and I didn't see her for more than a week during those six months."

Angela reached into her backpack and put a photograph on the table. "My mother," she said.

I could see a family resemblance. Her mother had dark hair and dark eyes like Angela, but that's where the similarity ended. The woman in the photo was...

"My mom was Lebanese," Angela said. "Her parents were killed when she was two months old. She was adopted. Her new parents immigrated to the U.S. when she was a baby. They named her Malak, which means angel. That's where I got my name."

I didn't take my eyes off the photo as Angela spoke. The woman in the photo did not look like an angel. She was lean and hard-muscled and a lot tougher looking than Angela. And it wasn't exactly the kind of photo you kept to remind you of your dead mother.

The photo had been taken at a firing range. Her mom was wearing a tank top, goggles, and ear protectors. She was shooting an automatic pistol at a target, but it wasn't the automatic or the muscles that made her look tough. There was an intensity in her eyes that I had never seen in Angela's eyes. The only feminine thing about her was the dainty gold necklace hanging around her neck. I thought about the woman in the photo being married to Roger and they didn't seem to match.

"Aside from protecting the president, the vice president, and their families," Angela continued, "the Service's primary duty is protecting U.S. currency. They work for the Treasury Department."

I looked up from the photo. Angela sounded like she could write a book about the subject. "So, they go after counterfeiters?"

Angela nodded. "But they also work with the FBI, the National Security Agency, Department of Defense, and Homeland Security. When she was killed she was working on an anti-terrorism task force from different agencies. At least that's what Dad thinks."

"He doesn't *know*?" I asked.

Angela shook her head.

"Why?"

"Classified information," Angela answered. "National security."

It was clear now why Mom didn't want me to bring up the subject. It also explained Mom's strange look and the change in mood when we were talking about James Bond novels in the café in Winnemucca. The Secret Service, whether it was the American or the British Secret Service, was obviously a sore subject for Roger.

"I'm sorry your mom died," I said, which seemed kind of lame, but I meant it. Losing your mother would be bad. Not knowing how or why would be horrible.

"Thanks," Angela said.

We sat for a few moments not saying anything. I glanced over at Boone to make sure he wasn't listening. He appeared to be engrossed in the radio show. The guy on the radio was talking about an encounter he had with an alien. I wondered if Boone believed in that stuff, or was just trying to stay awake. When I looked back, Angela was fiddling with the yellow origami crane.

"Dad wasn't happy about her being in the Service in the first place," she said quietly. "And then when they wouldn't give him any information about what happened, it just about put him over the edge."

"I can see that," I said. "It's outrageous. I mean it's not like he or you would give away national secrets."

"The point is that Dad's not exactly a big fan of federal law enforcement agencies," Angela said. "Which is why I don't talk about what I want to do when I grow up."

I stared at her for a minute, confused, until what she was talking about finally dawned on me.

"You mean you want to be a Secret Service agent?"

Angela nodded. "Or maybe FBI or CIA. I haven't decided yet."

I didn't know what to say.

"I know what you're thinking," Angela said. "You're wondering why I would want to join the same profession that took my mother."

That was a pretty good guess, but there was more to it than that. I was also thinking that Angela didn't look like she could ever be a federal agent or a spy. I mean she was fit enough, but there wasn't much to her. She was short, thin, and a little frail-looking.

"You're also probably wondering if I wanted to be an agent before my mom died or after she died," Angela said.

I hadn't even thought of that, but it was a good question.

"I don't know what she was doing, but I know it was something important," Angela continued. "And the answer is, yes. I wanted to be an agent before my mother died."

No wonder she hadn't told her dad. I bet he would let her eat an entire herd of cows if she promised to let this ambition go.

"Does he know that you've read all the James Bond novels?" I asked.

"No way."

"How do you become a federal agent, anyway?" I asked.

"Graduate from college of course, but while you're waiting you can work on your skills," Angela said. "Before Mom died she taught me a few things."

"Like what?"

"Like how to be observant, how to shake a tail, how to follow someone without being detected." Angela answered. "She made a game out of it—a private game that just she and I played."

"That's why you wear the sunglasses," I said.

Angela nodded. "Secret Service agents wear them when they're on protective duty so people don't know they're being watched."

"Did your dad know about these games?"

"I don't think so. Like I said, he wasn't happy about her being in the Service." Angela looked away. "And to be honest, before she disappeared, my mom and dad weren't getting along very well. Too many years apart with different outlooks and very different ambitions."

I knew something about this. My mom and my crazy dad had never gotten along.

"How did she teach you to be observant?" I asked.

"We'd go someplace like Chinatown in San Francisco, have lunch, and afterward she would quiz me on everyone sitting in the restaurant—what they were wearing, what they were eating, where they were sitting—"

"Two-hundred-fifty-six people at the wedding reception!" I said, "counting guests, catering staff, reporters, and security people. You actually counted them!"

"I guess I was showing off a little," Angela said.

"No more than when I made the burger wrapper disappear and turned it into the crane."

Angela was biting her lower lip again. There was more to come. I waited, but I guess she changed her mind.

"Show me how you did that trick," she said.

I knew this wasn't really what she wanted to say, but I let it go. She'd spill her guts when she was ready.

"Magicians aren't supposed to give away their secrets," I said. "But since you're my sister now I guess I can make an exception." I took out my deck of cards and gave it a one-handed shuffle. "I used distraction, sleight of hand, and anticipation."

"Explain," Angela said.

I reached under my leg and pulled out a crumpled yellow burger wrapper. "When I took the wrapper off I glanced at Boone and you looked in the same direction. That's the distraction. You only looked for a split second, but that's all I needed to flick the wrapper into my lap. That's the sleight of hand."

"How did you fold the crane so quickly?" she asked. "How did the crane get into the pocket of my robe?"

"That's the anticipation," I told her. "When I gave Croc his cheeseburger yesterday I pocketed the wrapper. I didn't think I'd be using it this soon, but I knew that one of these days you and I would be eating another McDonald's burger.

I took the wrapper and folded an origami crane when we got back to the coach. I was actually using it as a bookmark for *Dr. No*. When I saw that you were holding a burger for me I palmed the crane, then slipped it into your pocket when I followed you to the table."

"Clever," Angela said. "What about the disappearing French fries?"

"Sunglasses," I answered. "I asked you to take them off. People usually close their eyes or at least blink when they take off their glasses. That was enough time for me to flick the fries under the table."

Angela nodded and I thought the gut-spilling was going to come, but she still held back.

"What are *we* going to do on this tour?" she asked.

I shrugged. "I don't know. Hang out, do our homework."

"That's going to leave us a lot of time to ourselves," she said. "It's obvious that your mom and my dad are going to be a lot busier than they thought. Do you know other tricks?"

"Are you kidding?" I said. "I know hundreds of tricks. I've been doing magic since I was six years old."

I took out a length of cord and tied it in a complicated knot. I flicked it with my index finger and the knot disappeared.

Angela laughed, then said, "You know a lot about magic. I know something about being an agent. How about an exchange of information? You teach me some tricks and I'll teach you what my mom taught me."

"James Bond stuff," I said.

Angela nodded. "I can also teach you some taekwondo.

I've been taking lessons since I was four years old."

Looking at her, that was hard to believe.

"I get it," I said. "You teach me how to kick someone's head. I teach you how to *trick* someone's head."

Angela smiled. "Something like that."

The Electric Factory

We got to Philadelphia about three o'clock in the afternoon.

Boone pulled the coach into an old warehouse and Buddy jumped aboard before Boone had a chance to shut the engine off.

"You leave for New York in twenty minutes," he shouted.

"What?" Mom said.

"Private jet," Buddy continued. "We were lucky to get it. You'll be staying in a suite at Trump Tower. A driver will pick you up at six sharp tomorrow morning. Take you in for a sound check. The band's on its way to the airport. After you perform you fly to Chicago. After Chicago you—"

"Slow down Buddy," Roger said.

Angela closed her laptop. Boone unsnapped his seatbelt. I put my book down.

"We're on a tight schedule," Buddy continued. "Electric Factory concert is tomorrow night."

Boone got out of the driver's seat and stretched. He had been driving for over twenty-four hours, only taking breaks when we stopped to gas up.

"Hey, Boone," Buddy said, looking surprised. "When did you join up?"

Angela and I rolled our eyes. Like Buddy didn't know.

"Nevada," Boone answered.

"Great!" Buddy said. "I feel better with you behind the wheel. If you want to head up the roadies the job's yours."

"I'd be happy to give 'em a hand," Boone said. "But I got no interest in bein' the boss."

"Same old Boone," Buddy said. "I'll put you on the payroll."

Big surprise, I thought, and looked out the window. "Why are we parked in a warehouse?"

"It's perfect," Buddy answered. "Two blocks from The Electric Factory. I hired a security company to keep the fans away."

"We're staying here?" Angela asked.

"Yeah," Buddy said. "Your folks stipulated no hotels."

"Back up a little," Roger said. "What's this about a jet waiting for us?"

"I told you about it on the phone," Buddy said. "You're doing the Friday concert on *The Today Show* tomorrow morning. After you finish there you're flying to Chicago to do *Oprah*. We'll have you back here late Friday afternoon to get ready for your evening concert at the Electric Factory."

Roger and Mom looked at each other, stunned.

"You said you were working on *setting up* the appearances," Mom said. "You didn't say they were a done deal."

"They are now," Buddy said. "These two appearances

alone are going to sell a million albums—maybe more."

"What about Angela and Q?" Roger asked.

Buddy shook his head. "Corporate jet. Only a few seats. They're all taken. I can have one of the security guys drive them to New York and meet us. But then we have to figure out how to get them to Chicago and back to—"

"We'll stay here," Angela said, looking at me.

"Yeah," I agreed (a little quicker than I should have as it turned out).

"We can't have you staying here by yourselves," Roger said.

"It's only one night," Angela said. "Boone's here and there are guards. Besides we have a lot of homework to do. We can't be flying around with you every time you get a chance like this."

We didn't have that much homework. What did Angela have in mind? I wondered.

"What do you think?" Mom asked Roger.

"She has a point," Roger admitted. "But this isn't exactly how I envisioned the tour working out."

"Better get used to it," Buddy said. "You've hit the big time. You either take advantage of it or you give it up. You can't say no to things like this. They don't call you back to reschedule. They'll get some other act to perform and that act will sell a million albums."

Boone went over to the refrigerator and poured himself a glass of orange juice. "I don't mind hangin' with Angela and Q," he said. "We'll go to some bookstores, visit a coupla' museums…"

"I can't ask you to do that," Roger said. "You're not their

nanny."

Boone laughed. "You're right. I'm their friend. I like hangin' with them."

Buddy looked out the window. "Limo's here. We gotta go."

"Are you sure you'll be all right?" Mom asked me.

"Yeah," I said, trying to sound upbeat. "How about getting us cell phones and you can check in whenever you want?" I'd been bugging her about getting a cell phone for over a year. Angela wanted one too.

Mom smiled and looked at Roger.

"It's okay with me," he said.

She looked at Boone. "Do you think you can arrange to get these two cell phones?"

"No problem," Boone said.

"Let me give you a credit card," Roger said, reaching for his wallet.

"Don't worry about it," Boone said. "We'll settle up later."

"Great!" Buddy said. "Everything's taken care of. Pack some clothes. Let's go."

Within minutes Mom and Roger were out of the coach, climbing into a white stretch limousine with Buddy.

Mom lowered the tinted window as they rolled out of the warehouse. "Call us as soon as you get the phones!"

"Stay out of trouble!" Roger said.

"We love you!" they both said.

The limo took off down the street.

"I'm gonna get some shut-eye," Boone said. "We'll go out and get your cells when I wake up." He walked back into the coach.

I looked at Angela. "Why didn't you want to go with them?"

"It's our only chance to see Philadelphia," she said. "And I didn't feel like going for a drive with a security guard. Let's go in and get our homework out of the way."

At least I was getting a cell phone out of the deal.

Cells

While Boone prowled yet another bookstore, Angela and I sat in a little restaurant down the street figuring out how to use our new cell phones, which were actually "smart phones" that had E-mail, web browsing, and cameras. The phones even had a built-in Global Positioning System in case we got lost. I would have settled for a little flip phone, but Boone insisted that we get a phone just like he had. It was called a BlackBerry. Which was interesting, because before we got to the store, I didn't even know he had a cell phone.

Ever since we'd left the warehouse, I noticed that Angela had been acting a little strange. She was quieter than usual, which meant she had hardly spoken a word. If she kept this up it was going to be a very long weekend and I was beginning to really regret not going to New York.

We called our parents, got their voice mail, and left them messages. I ordered a roast beef sandwich and Angela ordered fish and chips for dinner, which she didn't touch. She was too busy memorizing everyone in the restaurant with her shades on even though it had been dark outside for hours. Halfway through my sandwich she took off her sunglasses and bit her lower lip. Finally, I thought.

"I didn't tell you everything last night," she said.

I tried to act surprised.

"You'll think I'm crazy," she continued.

I shook my head.

She took a deep breath, held it a second, then let it out quickly in one long sentence: "For the past few weeks I've had the feeling that I'm being followed. At first I thought I was just being paranoid–that the feeling was because of all the attention my dad and Blaze were getting, but now I *know* someone's following me."

She was right. I did think she was crazy.

"Who?" I asked.

Angela put her sunglasses back on. "Don't stare, but there's a man across the street standing by the dry cleaner."

I glanced out the window. Sure enough there was a man standing in front of the dry cleaner under a streetlight. There were also three kids doing wheelies on their skateboards, a woman pushing a stroller, and another man sipping a cup of coffee, sitting on a bench and enjoying the cool night air.

"So?" I said.

"He followed us from the warehouse to the cell phone store, then he followed us over here."

"Could be a coincidence."

"He was also at the wedding reception at Golden Gate Park."

That got my attention. I glanced back over at him. "Are

you sure?"

"Positive," Angela said. "Let me see your camera."

I fished it out of my pocket and gave it to her. She went through the photos one by one. "Right there," she said, handing it back.

I looked at the image. There were about thirty people in the picture. The lighting was terrible. A half-dozen of them could have been the man standing across the street.

Angela pointed to one of the half-dozen. I zoomed in on him. It was possible, but the picture was so distorted I couldn't tell.

"Why would someone be following you?"

"That's just it," Angela said. "I don't know."

"Maybe he's one of Buddy's security guys."

"Buddy didn't send security all the way from San Francisco," Angela said. "The guards at the warehouse are wearing uniforms. And they wouldn't be sneaking around. What would be the point?"

The guy standing next to the dry cleaner wasn't sneaking around, he was standing out in the open right under a light, but her point about the uniforms was good. The guy had on a flannel shirt and jeans. But I still thought she was crazy.

I shook my head. "I don't remember seeing him at the wedding."

Angela gave me an angry glare. "He wasn't dressed like that." She took her sunglasses off, grabbed her pack, and stood up.

"What are you doing?"

"I'm going to walk around the block," she said. "If he

doesn't follow me, then I am crazy."

"And if he does?"

"Maybe then you'll believe me!"

She stomped out of the restaurant.

My new sister was paranoid and touchy.

I thought about going with her, but I really didn't think the guy was going to follow her. I watched him as I ate Angela's fries. He looked in the direction she had gone, but he didn't move. I was confident he'd be standing right where he was when she came around the block—with her senses back, I hoped.

As I popped the third fry into my mouth Mr. Flannel Shirt took his cell phone out and made a call. On the fourth fry he started across the street toward the restaurant and walked right past the window where I was sitting. I felt a stab of fear. Up close he did look a little like the guy at the wedding. He had dark hair and hadn't shaved in several days, but the thing that bothered me the most was his eyes. There was something feral and predatory about them. If he wasn't hunting Angela, he was certainly after something. I got up and was halfway to the door when I remembered our BlackBerrys.

Angela answered on the second ring.

"I think he's following you," I said, stepping outside. The man was fifty yards down the block, moving quickly. There was no sign of Angela.

"I told you," Angela said.

"He looks like a mugger," I said.

"I'll be fine," Angela said. "And he's not a mugger. A few days ago he was serving drinks at the wedding."

"Well today I think he's serving trouble." I looked around and noticed Croc was gone. "Is Croc with you?"

"Right at my heels," Angela said.

"Pick up your pace," I said. "I'm going to go around the block the other way and meet you. Don't hang–" My phone beeped. I looked at the screen. "My mom's calling."

"Don't tell her what's going on," Angela said.

"That shouldn't be a problem," I said. "Since I don't know what is going on!"

I picked up the incoming call as I started walking.

"Hi, Q," Mom said. "How's everything in the City of Brotherly Love?"

"Great. How's it going in the Big Apple?"

"New York City is insane! When we landed there must have been fifty photographers and reporters waiting for us. A caravan of paparazzi followed our limo, led by our annoying friend, Dirk Peski. His interview in Grand Island made a big splash and he's attached to us like a parasite. We've done five interviews in the last five hours and there are more television crews waiting in the hallway. I had to hide out in the bathroom to make this call."

Mom was about as wound up as I'd ever heard her. And the timing could not have been worse.

"Roger and I talked about it on the way to Trump Tower," she continued as I hurried down the block, phone to my ear. "The tour's already out of control and it hasn't actually started. We're worried about you and Angela."

"There's nothing to worry about here," I said. "Everything's fine. We're with Boone and we have our cell phones if you–"

"Thank God for Boone!" Mom said. "And speaking of cell phones, Roger and I are getting our numbers changed. Our numbers were put out on the Internet. We're getting calls from complete strangers. I'll give you the new numbers as soon as we have them. Buddy's hired personal assistants for us to return calls and to take care of all the other stuff we don't have time for. Once the PAs are in place I'm sure things will settle down."

"The PAs are a good idea," I said. I reached the corner expecting to see Angela hurrying toward me. She wasn't there!

"Where are you?" Mom asked.

"Uh... I'm headed over to the bookstore where Boone and Angela are."

"Oh good," Mom said. "I want to talk to Boone."

"I'll have him call you," I said.

"I'll wait," Mom said. "I have a few minutes before the next interview..."

I took a closer look at my so-called *corner*, and with great relief, realized that it wasn't a corner, it was an alley. Angela wouldn't cut through a dark alley strewn with dumpsters and trash. I hurried down the block.

"Roger's doing a sound check at Rockefeller Center..." Mom continued. "I hate to admit it, Q, but I'm really nervous about the concert tomorrow. And you know me...I never get stage fright."

That was true, but I didn't have time to talk about it. I reached the end of the block, turned the real corner, and nearly tripped over Croc. Angela wasn't with him. It was all I could do not to scream and tip off my mother.

"Are you there yet?" Mom asked.

"Uh... you're breaking up. I think I'm walking through a dead zone," I said, hoping I wasn't being literal. "Are you there?"

"I can hear you clear as a bell," Mom said, as clear as a bell.

"What?"

Sorry Mom, I thought, but I've just lost my new sister and your new daughter. I hit the end button.

"Where is she?" I asked Croc.

He gave me a goofy toothless grin.

I called Angela's cell.

"Hi, this is Angela. Leave a message."

Beep.

"Where are you?" I shouted.

"Problem?"

This time there wasn't a bowl of cereal to spill when I jumped. I wished Boone would quit sneaking up on me. If he kept this up I was going to start calling him Boo instead of Boone. But I was relieved to see him.

"Yeah, there's a *problem,*" I said, but before I could explain, my phone rang again. "Hello?"

"Can you hear me now?" Mom asked.

I was tempted to hang up. "Kind of," I said.

"Did you make it to the bookstore? And what are you doing running around the street after dark? Where is Boone?"

I sighed in defeat. "He's standing right next to me." I gave Boone my BlackBerry.

It's over, I thought. In a second Mom will know that we

weren't at the bookstore and that something was seriously wrong. She and Roger will abandon the tour, grab us on their way west, and Angela will hate me for the rest of her life, which could be relatively short if Mr. Flannel Shirt was actually after her.

"Evenin' Blaze," Boone said. "That's right. Angela? She's upstairs lookin' at history books about Philadelphia for their assignment…"

I stared at Boone in complete shock. He was lying so convincingly *I* almost believed we were in a bookstore and not standing on a street corner.

"Right…" he continued. "No, we're good here. Havin' a great time. We're gonna catch a movie later… I just sent Q across the street to see what time it started. I will… Right… If we're watchin' a movie their phones won't be on. Just leave a message when you get your new cell numbers. Okay, talk to you later." Boone pushed the end button and handed the phone back. "What's going on?" he asked.

I told him everything.

Boone wasn't nearly as surprised as I thought he'd be. In fact he looked kind of amused as I recounted what had happened. When I finished he said, "I think Angela is fine."

"Then where is she?" I asked, looking down at Croc, who had the same amused expression as Boone. "Croc was with her. Now he's here."

"Call her," Boone said.

I called her. She answered on the first ring.

"Where are you?" she asked, sounding irritated.

Mars, I thought. "Where are you?"

"I'm at the restaurant. I thought you were going to meet me around the block."

"I went around the block and I called."

"I was talking to my dad," Angela said. "I just got off the phone with him. He was on his way back to the hotel from *The Today Show* studio. I was about to call you."

I was getting more confused by the second. "What about the guy?"

"He's back at the dry cleaner."

Croc walked over to a fire hydrant and took a pee. "I thought you said Croc was with you."

"He was," Angela said. "When I got back to the restaurant he ran off. Is he with you?"

"Yeah, so is Boone."

"Don't tell him about any of this," Angela said.

Too late, I thought. But it could have been worse. I'd nearly spilled my guts to my mom. "We'll be there in a minute," I said and clicked off.

The grin on Boone's face was really starting to bug me.

"What's so funny?" I asked.

He shrugged.

"Where did you come from?" I asked.

"The bookstore," Boone answered.

"Then where are the books?" Boone had his little daypack slung over his shoulder, which was too full to hold books. He always carried the books he bought in grocery sacks. "You lied to my mom pretty smoothly."

"You didn't do too bad yourself," Boone said.

I stared at him and suddenly realized that Boone was not

who he said he was. He had lied about everything.

"Who are you?" I asked.

"An ancient roadie."

I shook my head. "I don't think so."

Boone shrugged again.

"Buddy didn't ask you to follow us did he?"

Boone was silent.

"There was no young guitar player with you when you found us broke down on the side of the road," I continued. "You knew Q stood for Quest."

"I guess you caught me," Boone said without a hint of remorse. Also missing was the southern drawl. Now he no longer sounded like the Boone I knew.

I repeated his words in the motor home, imitating his fake accent. "I'm their friend. I like hangin' with them."

"I am your friend," Boone said quietly.

"What do you want with us?" I asked.

Boone looked at me a moment before answering. "Let's go back to the restaurant and I'll tell you and Angela at the same time," he said. "I don't want to explain it twice."

"Fine," I said.

Spook

We joined Angela at a table near the window.

"Hi, Boone," Angela said with a big fake smile like everything was perfect. "How was the bookstore?"

Boone returned the smile, but didn't answer the question.

Angela turned her smile on me. "I went around the block across the street," she said. "You must have gone around this block. That's why we missed each other." She looked back at Boone. "We were testing our new phones."

"Boone knows," I said.

Angela continued to smile, which meant she didn't know what Boone knew or what I was talking about.

"The phones work great," she continued to Boone. "But you already know that because you have one."

"It's not exactly like yours," Boone said.

"Turns out that Boone isn't *exactly* who he says he is, either," I said, a little more harshly than I intended.

Angela stopped smiling. "Did I miss something?" she asked.

"Yeah," I said. "And so did I."

"What are you talking about?"

"Buddy didn't hire Boone to drive the coach," I said. "That was Boone's idea." I glanced out the window at Mr. Flannel Shirt. "I told Boone about the guy following you and he didn't act too surprised. Do you know why?"

Angela shook her head.

"I don't know either," I said. "But if I had to guess I would say that Boone already knew he was following you."

Angela frowned. "Did you–"

"Tell Boone about your mom?" I said. "Yeah. But only because I thought you were in trouble. Boone promised that he would explain everything when we got back to the restaurant." I looked at Boone. "We're here."

"Are you sure you're ready for all this?" Boone asked.

Angela and I nodded.

"The man across the street is a spook for Israeli intelligence," Boone said with an absolute straight face.

"A spook?" I said.

"Spy," Boone clarified.

"Oh yeah," I scoffed.

"You mean the Mossad?" Angela asked, acting as if Boone were telling the truth.

Boone nodded. "In Hebrew Mossad means 'The Institute.' It's the Institute for Intelligence and Special Operations, equivalent to our Central Intelligence Agency, or MI6 in the United Kingdom."

I thought Boone and Angela were both crazy. "Let me get this straight," I said. "Are you saying the guy in the flannel shirt is an actual spy?"

"Big-time spy," Boone said. "And an assassin. His name is Eben Lavi."

"You've been reading too many Spy-Fi novels," I said.

"You know him?" Angela asked.

It was like I wasn't there. I was about ready to scream.

"I don't know him," Boone said. "But I know a lot about him. He's an anti-terrorist specialist. One of the best in the business...or was. I'm not sure what his current status is."

"How do you know any of this?" I asked.

"Why would he be following me?" Angela asked.

"I'm not sure why he's following you," Boone said to Angela.

Angela gave me a triumphant glare. "I told you he was following me!"

Just because an ancient roadie said it was true didn't mean it was true, I thought.

"I could feel him watching me," Angela continued. "Even back in San Francisco before I spotted him here I knew people were watching me." She looked out the window at Mr. Flannel Shirt. "I don't think Eben Lavi is very good at this."

"That depends on what he's trying to do," Boone said.

"What do you mean?" Angela asked.

"Maybe he's trying to intimidate you. Maybe he's trying to get you to run to your parents, hoping they'll quit the tour and go home. It would be much easier to keep an eye on you if you weren't moving from city to city." Boone paused and glanced across the street. "Or maybe it's something entirely different."

I was a lot more interested in how Boone knew all this and where his accent had gone than I was in what he thought Mr. Flannel Shirt did for a living. I wondered if Angela had noticed that Boone wasn't dropping his g's anymore.

"Why don't we walk across the street and ask him?" I said.

Boone looked at me like *I* was crazy.

"I don't think that's a good idea," he said.

I didn't think it was a good idea either, but I had finally gotten his attention. "How do you know that's Eben Lavi?" I asked.

"I studied his dossier," Boone said. "I used to work for the CIA."

"You were a spook?" Angela raised her voice and several people looked our way.

Boone held his index finger to his bearded lips and nodded. "Once upon a time," he said.

Once Upon a Time

Tyrone Boone was recruited by the Central Intelligence Agency in his senior year of college.

"I was a NOC agent," he explained. "Non-Official Cover. I operated off the books. Which means that no one knew I worked for the CIA–including all but a handful of people within the CIA. Being a roadie was the perfect cover. It allowed me to travel all over the world with electronic surveillance equipment, which I smuggled into countries as sound and special-effects equipment for the shows."

After thirty years as a spy he retired, built a little house on the California coast at Big Sur, and planned to spend the rest of his life watching seabirds soar over the Pacific.

"But plans change," he said. "The twin towers came crashing down in New York City."

"You went back to work for the CIA," Angela said.

"No," Boone said. "I'd had enough of bureaucratic incompetence. The intelligence community is a culture of absolute paranoia. The CIA doesn't trust the FBI, the FBI doesn't trust the CIA, neither of them trust the National Security Agency, the NSA doesn't trust the Mossad, the Mossad doesn't trust MI6 in Britain... No one trusts anyone—sometimes with good reason—and as a result nothing gets done.

"I didn't want to get caught up in this swirl of stupidity again so I put together a team of my own. We contract our services out. Or we look into things that interest us for free. Either way we act independently without somebody in a suit breathing down our necks. In other words, we actually manage to gather valuable intelligence from time to time."

"What do you do with the intelligence?" Angela asked.

"That depends," Boone said. "Most of the time we pass it along to government agencies." He paused. "All of them, at the exact same time without regard to borders, except for the current bad guys of course. One of the problems is that when the CIA, Secret Service, FBI, or the National Security Agency learn something, they don't share the information outside their organizations, and definitely not outside the U.S. They're like a kindergartner with a new toy. We force them to play together by making sure they all have the same toy at the same time."

"What does this have to do with me?" Angela asked.

"How did you find us in the middle of the desert in Nevada?" I asked, desperately trying to inject some reality into the conversation.

Boone looked at us for a moment. "I'll answer Q's question first because it's the easiest to deal with," he said. "But you're not going to like the answer. I put a device on your coach and rigged it to cause a breakdown at a certain time."

The first thing I thought was, *car bomb!* Angela looked just as alarmed as I felt.

"I told you that you weren't going to like the answer," Boone said. "It would have been a lot easier if your parents had taken on a driver, like Buddy wanted. I had it all arranged."

"We could have been hurt!" Angela said.

Boone shook his head. "Unlikely. It was just a little something on your fuel system that cut off the diesel supply."

"Does Buddy know about you being a spy?" Angela asked.

"He would be the last person I would tell," Boone answered. "But he did suggest I try to talk Blaze into taking me on as a driver."

"So you followed us and ditched your car," I said.

"It turned out to be a little more involved than that," Boone said. "You see, when I put my little device under your rig in San Rafael I discovered someone else's tracking device. It took us awhile to figure out who put it there."

"Eben Lavi," Angela said.

"Right," Boone said.

"Why didn't you just take the tracking thing off?" I asked, still skeptical of this whole thing.

"I could have, but sometimes it's better to wait. It gave me a chance to track them without them knowing they were being tracked. You can learn a lot that way. Unfortunately, I had to change plans in Nevada."

"What happened?" Angela asked.

Boone smiled. "I was following them following you, but I couldn't have them find you broken down in the desert.

Luckily, they stopped for something to eat. I stole their car and had them picked up by the police. The delay put them behind us by several hours. Eben flew to Philly when they got to Salt Lake City. And their driver got to the city ahead of us.

Boone took out his BlackBerry and punched a couple of buttons. He showed us the screen. There was a little red arrow heading east on Interstate 80.

If this was a hoax, it was a pretty elaborate one. I wasn't as convinced as Angela seemed to be, but I was starting to have second thoughts.

"You put a tracking device on Eben's car," I said.

Boone nodded.

"You've answered Q's question," Angela said. "What about my question?"

Boone glanced across the street at Eben then he stared down at the table for a long time at nothing in particular. Finally, he sighed, raised his pale gray eyes, and locked them on Angela.

"I think there is a 50/50 chance that your mother is still alive," he said.

Charade

"What?" Angela whispered.

I was surprised that she could even get that much out. I was speechless.

"50/50 chance," Boone emphasized. "I think that's why Eben's following you."

"And this is why you're with us," Angela said quietly.

"I'll tell you more about that later," Boone said, looking at his watch. "Right now we have to be somewhere, but first we have to shake your tail." He pressed a button on his BlackBerry and held it to his ear. "Are you ready? Good. We'll be right out..."

"Wait a second!" I said. "Who were you talking to? What do you mean, 'we'll be right out'?"

Boone was halfway out of his chair. He sat back down. "Q, you're just going to have to trust me," he said.

"Well I don't," I said. "Why should I?"

"Fair enough," Boone said calmly. "I'm sorry for the charade, but you'll come to see that it was necessary. I can't tell you another thing about Angela's mother, or anything else, until I'm certain you and Angela are one hundred percent with me on this. And I'll be the one to determine whether you are with me or not. You're either in or you're out.

"I'm going outside to distract our friend." He nodded toward the door at the back of the restaurant. "That door leads to a service alley. Leave the restaurant separately. Angela, you go first. There's a produce truck parked there. I want you to climb into the back of the truck. If you don't get in the truck, I'm gone. You won't have to worry about whether you trust me or not. You will never see me again." He got up and walked out.

"This is crazy," I said, getting out my phone.

"What are you doing?" Angela asked.

"Calling Mom."

"No," Angela said. She looked numb.

"Boone...is...a...nut...case," I said slowly. "Did you happen to notice that he sounded like an entirely different human being? I think he has some kind of split personality."

"I think he's telling the truth," Angela said quietly.

"Even if he is, this is still crazy. We can't climb into the back of a produce truck in an alley and be driven off to who knows where. What if *Boone* and Mr. Flannel Shirt are working together? What if Boone is the bad guy in all of this? What if this is just an elaborate setup? What if he's trying to kidnap us?"

"There are a lot easier ways to kidnap us than this," Angela said. "He and whoever he's working with could have abducted us anytime this evening." She pointed to my phone. "Do you think he'd leave us in a public place with two cell phones if he wanted to kidnap us?"

I looked down at my phone.

"If you tell your mom," Angela continued, "it's all over. They'll cancel the tour. And I'll never find out what happened to my mother." She stood up. "I'm going to get into a produce truck in an alley to be driven off to who knows where. You can do whatever you want. But I'm going to find out if my mother is still alive." She walked over to the back door and disappeared through it without looking back.

This is stupid! I thought.

I called Mom. She answered on the fourth ring.

"Hi, Q!"

"Hi, Mom."

"The interviews are over," she said. "Thank God! And Buddy's found us a place to rehearse, so we should be in good shape for tomorrow's appearance. Roger and the band are already over there setting up the equipment. My new PA, Marie, and I are just finished doing some shopping. We found a couple of great outfits for tomorrow."

"I bet they're red," I said.

Mom laughed. "As a matter of fact they are. We're in the limo headed to the rehearsal hall. Traffic's terrible! What movie are you going to see?"

James Bond, I thought. I pictured her in the back of that limo getting ready to sing in front of millions of people and I could feel her excitement. I pictured Angela sitting in the back of a produce truck and I could feel how ticked off she was at me.

"We don't know yet," I said. "We're about ready to head

over to the theater. I was just checking in to see how you're doing."

"I'm a little tired," Mom said. "But I'm looking forward to tomorrow. By the way, the satellite television in the coach won't work inside the warehouse. If you want to see us you'll have to get Boone to take you someplace where you can watch the show tomorrow morning. We're performing at the end of the first and second hours. But don't worry if you miss it. We'll get a tape."

Boone might have a TV in the room where he'll be holding us hostage, I thought.

"We'll find a television," I said.

"Hang on…" Mom said. I could hear another woman talking in the background. "Oh all right… Marie tells me that we're here, Q. I better go. Don't stay up too late and be good. I love you."

"I love you too."

I looked out the window. Eben Lavi was looking at his cell phone. He flipped it closed, put it back in his pocket, then leaned against the building with his arms across his chest as if he didn't have a care in the world. I didn't see Boone anywhere.

Mr. Little

Angela was sitting on a box of lettuce. Croc was leaning on a box of bananas. I sat on a box of apples across from them. An old woman wearing a green smock pulled the door closed with barely a glance. It was so dark inside I couldn't see Angela. The latch clanged into place and it occurred to me that not only was I being forced to eat vegetables I was now being voluntarily kidnapped by vegetables. I guess I was a little hysterical because as the truck rumbled out of the alley I started laughing. When I finally stopped I heard Angela crying. I thought they were tears of regret. That she had finally realized what a boneheaded move we had just made. I reached out and tried to find her hand and found Croc's tongue instead.

"Don't worry," I said, wiping Croc's goo on my cargoes. "As soon as they stop we'll jump out and run. The old woman who locked us in didn't look that fast."

"I just don't understand how she could do something like that?" Angela said tearfully.

"You mean the old woman?"

"No," Angela said. "How could my mom leave me and Dad? How could she let us think that she was dead?"

I guess she hadn't been crying because we had just made the biggest mistake of our lives.

"What kind of mother would do something like that?" she asked.

I didn't have any answers for her, but I did think about her question and came up with a few questions of my own: If Angela's mom was still alive was my mom really married to Roger? Was Roger my stepfather? Was Angela my stepsister? Was Boone really a former spy?

The truck came to a stop less than ten minutes after we started. Boone slid the door open.

"Let's go," he said and started across the dark street with Croc at his heels.

I still couldn't get over his personality transformation. He was like Dr. Jekyll and Mr. Hyde. As soon as we got out, the truck took off.

"I guess we're not being kidnapped," Angela said, pointing to Boone.

He was heading straight for the most famous brick building in the United States—Independence Hall. I recognized it because we had written about it on our Web page that afternoon. This was the place where George Washington was appointed commander in chief of the Continental Army in 1775 and the Declaration of Independence was adopted in 1776.

"Yeah," I said. "But what are we doing here? It's closed."

"I guess we'll find out," Angela said. Except for a little redness around her eyes she seemed to have recovered. "And do me a favor," she added. "Don't even mention my mother to Boone. Let him bring the subject up when he's ready."

"Whatever," I said, still thinking this whole cloak-and-dagger thing was ridiculous.

"I mean it, Q!" Angela insisted. "I think Boone is having second thoughts about all this. I don't want him to abandon us without finding out what he knows about my mother."

"All right," I said. "I'll keep my mouth shut. But I still think this is nuts."

Without breaking stride, Boone turned his head and said, "Hurry up, we need to get off the street."

We got to the back entrance of Independence Hall just as the door was opened by a man in a three-piece suit. Standing next to him was a giant uniformed guard.

"Are you Mr. Boone?" the man in the suit asked with undisguised disapproval.

"Yes," Boone said.

"My name is Neville Little. I am the superintendent of the Independence Hall National Historical Park." He nodded at the giant guard. "And this is our head of security, Brod Bagert. I'm sorry, but we're going to need to see some identification."

Boone impatiently pulled his wallet out of his hip pocket and handed a laminated card to him. Mr. Little scrutinized the card as if it contained the entire text of the Declaration of Independence.

Boone looked over his shoulder at the street, then back at Mr. Little. "Could we hurry this up?"

"We're just being cautious," Mr. Little said.

"That's great, but could we be cautious inside?"

Brod stood up a little straighter and his right hand dropped toward the black automatic hanging on his belt.

Mr. Little gave the card back in slow motion then looked down at Croc with distaste. "I'm afraid we don't allow dogs inside Independence Hall, unless of course they are service dogs, which he obviously is not."

Apparently Boone's *disguise* didn't always work to his advantage, but he had a way around that. He whipped out his phone and hit a speed dial button.

"It's Boone," he said, not taking his eyes off the superintendent. "Yeah…well, Mr. Neville Little, superintendent of the Independence Hall National Historical Park, doesn't seem to understand the gravity of the situation… Yes, he's standing right here with a security guard who looks like he's about to pull his gun on us… Sure." Boone handed the BlackBerry to Mr. Little. "It's for you."

Mr. Little held the phone to his ear. I couldn't hear who was on the other end, but it was clearly someone Mr. Little knew. His eyes widened and his face turned as red as the building's bricks. "Yes sir," he said, handing the phone back with a lot less bluster than he'd had a moment before.

Boone slipped the BlackBerry into his pocket without even bothering to check if whoever was on the other end was still on the line. He started through the door, but Brod stepped in front of him.

"No!" Mr. Little shrieked. "It's okay. They're all welcome inside. Including the dog."

Croc's nails clicked on the old wooden floor as we followed Mr. Little and the guard down a narrow hallway.

"I think we have everything set up per your instructions," Mr. Little said, as he led us up a set of stairs. "I've dismissed all the security people except for Brod. He'll be manning the front desk alone tonight and will stay out of your way."

"Good," Boone said curtly.

I still wasn't convinced that Boone was a former spy, but he was obviously someone with influential friends. Mr. Little was now fluttering around him like a nervous butterfly. Brod still looked suspicious.

"I've set you up in the conference room," Mr. Little said, unlocking a door.

Inside was a long rustic table surrounded by vintage chairs. Hanging on one of the walls was a large mirror mounted in an ornate gilded frame. Beneath it was an old overstuffed love-seat. Sitting on the table was a television with a built-in DVD player, which looked totally out of place among the antiques.

"This is not a playroom," Mr. Little said, eyeing Angela and me. "The table and chairs are some of the original furniture from the Hall."

He turned to Brod. "I guess you'd better get back down to the front desk."

Brod looked at Boone. "I switched the cameras off like Mr. Little requested. How long will they be off?"

"A couple of hours. We'll let you know when you can turn them back on. Don't let anyone inside. And I don't care who they say they are. Is that clear?"

Brod gave Boone a surly nod and left the room.

"I appreciate your time, Mr. Little," Boone said. "We can handle it from here."

"Of course," Mr. Little said. "I'll be in my office if you need–"

Boone shook his head. "I'm afraid you'll have to leave the building too. National security."

Mr. Little turned bright red in outrage, but recovered quickly. "Of course. I'll just get my things."

As soon as Mr. Little left, Boone pulled out some kind of electronic gadget from his pack and started running it along the walls.

"What are you doing?" Angela asked.

"Sweeping the room for listening devices," Boone said. "It's not likely there are any, but you never know."

"Why are we at Independence Hall?" I asked.

"You are here for a history lesson," Boone said. "But it's not one you will be putting on your Web page, or telling another living soul about...ever."

Cat and Mouse

"Take a seat," Boone said.

Angela and I sat down across from him.

"We have to wait a few minutes to make sure Mr. Little is out of here and the building is secure," Boone said. "While we're waiting let me see your BlackBerrys."

We gave them to him. He opened the backs of both phones and removed the thumbnail-sized SIM cards they had installed at the phone store and tossed them in the garbage.

"I thought those were what made the phones work," I said.

"They are," Boone said. "But to make your phones really smart we need these special SIMs." He pulled a small plastic bag from his shirt pocket, and with a pair of tweezers from his Swiss Army Knife took out two new SIM cards. He carefully inserted the SIMs and turned the BlackBerrys back on.

"With these I can keep track of you and you can keep track of me." He slid the phones back over to us. "If you push the tracking icon you'll see a list of people."

I looked at the screen menu. There were twelve people listed including Boone, Angela, and me.

"The one named Ziv is Eben's driver," Boone said. "We have a tracking device on his SUV, but I don't know how long that will last. They'll discover the device eventually and take it off. Eben's with Ziv now. The other seven people are members of my team. Five are here in Philly. The other two will be here tomorrow afternoon."

I clicked on Ziv. He and Eben were a few blocks away from the restaurant moving east–or at least their SUV was.

I clicked Boone's name, then my own name, then Angela's. We were all in the exact same spot. I clicked back to Ziv.

"I'm sure Eben has other assets on the ground," Boone continued. "But we haven't spotted them yet. So, you need to be very careful. It could be anybody. One of the security guards at the warehouse. One of the roadies working for the show…

"There's another icon you need to know about–SOS. It's a distress signal, but it doesn't go to the police. Don't hesitate to push it if you're in trouble, or even if you feel threatened. Within a minute, or probably seconds, someone from the team will be there to help you."

"What about my dad and Blaze?" Angela asked. "Are they in any danger?"

I hadn't even thought about Roger or Mom being in trouble. But again, I still wasn't one hundred percent convinced that Boone was telling the truth.

"Until they left for New York I didn't know if Eben was following you, your dad, or both of you," Boone said. "If he was following your dad he would have gone to New York. I think they're fine. But as a precaution we have people watching them. The two personal assistants Buddy hired to help them actually work for me. Your parents don't know it, but they now have PAs *and* personal bodyguards."

"What's my mom's bodyguard's name?" I asked suspiciously. Angela kicked me under the table. I ignored the attack.

"Her name is Marie," Boone answered. "And don't let the gender fool you. Marie is tougher than Roger's bodyguard, whose name, by the way is, Art. You can find out where they are by clicking their names on your BlackBerrys. They'll be watching your parents' backs 24/7. By tomorrow your parents will also be listed on your BlackBerrys, so you can keep track of them."

"Can they track us?" Angela asked.

Boone shook his head. "They don't have the same SIM card in their BlackBerrys."

I was glad to hear that. I didn't want Mom to know where I was every second of the day, but it was going to be fun knowing where she was.

"If Eben is after Angela why didn't he try to follow her when she left the restaurant out the back door," I asked. This warranted another kick from Angela, but I didn't care. "All he had to do was call one of his people to pick her up," I continued. "Ziv can't be driving their only car. Before I left I saw Eben slip his phone back into his pocket. He didn't look like he was going anywhere."

"Eben tried to make a phone call," Boone said. "But he

wasn't able to get a cell signal because I jammed it with this."
He pulled another gadget out of his pack. "We were hoping
he'd make a mistake and lead us to the other people he's
working with. But he's a professional. As soon as I jammed his
phone he knew he'd been made. He also knew that he wasn't
dealing with the security detail Buddy hired. They don't have
this kind of gear. He stayed exactly where he was and waited
for Ziv to show up."

I looked down at my phone. "Speaking of which, the car
has stopped."

Boone nodded.

"Hey!" I said. "The signal just went out."

"Eben just found the tracking device and crushed it,"
Boone said. "He and Ziv will split up and try to lose us and
at the same time try to figure out who we are. It's a cat-and-
mouse game." He looked at Angela. "This is why you need to
be very careful."

Angela bit her lower lip. She was about to go against
her own advice and ask him about her mother. I jumped in
before the dam broke. "Who was the guy you talked to on the
phone?"

"Mr. Potus," Boone said. "And that's all you need to know
about him, so don't ask again."

"Okay," I said.

Boone grabbed his pack and stood up. "I'm going to look
around. You two stay here. And stay away from the window."
He walked out of the room with Croc at his heels.

"Do you believe Boone now?" Angela asked.

"Yep," I said, but I was actually only about ninety-five percent convinced. "And you're welcome."

"For what?" Angela asked.

"For me stopping you from asking Boone about your mother."

"I wasn't going to ask him about my mother," Angela said.

I imitated her biting her lower lip.

"Yes you were," I said.

She didn't argue so I knew I was right. "Here's a question," I said. "If your mom is alive are Roger and my mom legally married?"

"I thought about that," Angela said. "My mom was pronounced legally dead. If that's the case Blaze and my dad are legally married."

"Even if your mother isn't technically dead," I said.

"I think so," Angela said, but she didn't look sure and neither was I.

The Ghost Cell

"What are you doing?" Angela asked.

"Practicing."

I was standing in front of the ancient mirror trying to figure out how to palm my phone so nobody could see me take photos with it. The phone was bigger than the camera Mom had given me so it wasn't easy to hide in one hand. Also, the shutter release was going to be hard to reach without using my other hand, which would totally blow the trick. The problem was that my cargo pockets were getting a little crowded with the digital camera, BlackBerry, cord, decks of cards, and other gear. Something was going to have to go and I decided it would be the digital camera since the BlackBerry had a camera.

"Thanks for going along with this," Angela said. "I know you didn't want to."

I looked at her reflection in the mirror. "Do you think George Washington stared at himself in this mirror to make sure his false teeth were in place?"

"Maybe," Angela said. "What do you think Boone is doing right now?"

"I've given up on trying to figure out Tyrone Boone. That's probably not even his real name. Have you thought of that?"

I managed to do a one-handed shutter release. I checked the picture. It was a photo of me and Angela reflected in the mirror, blurry, but recognizable.

I showed it to Angela. "Not too bad considering it was an accident."

"Not too good either," Angela said.

Boone and Croc came back into the room. Boone sat down. Croc jumped up on a rickety loveseat along the wall and began grooming his nether region. If Mr. Little saw this he would have had a coronary.

Boone set a small digital tape recorder on the table and looked at Angela. "I need to ask you some questions. Can I record you?"

"I guess," Angela said, looking a little nervous.

Boone switched the recorder on. "If you don't mind I'm going to refer to your mother by her given name."

"All right," Angela said.

"What did the Secret Service tell you about Malak's death?"

I guess Boone, the spook, didn't believe in easing into things.

Angela took a deep breath. "They said that she was killed by a suicide bomber overseas."

"Did they tell you where?"

Angela shook her head. "They said they couldn't reveal

the location because of national security."

"When did they say she was killed?"

"November 30, 2004."

"At least they gave you the right date," Boone said.

"But you said my mother was alive," Angela said.

Boone held his hand up. "Let's get through this before we get into that."

I sat down and took out my deck of cards. Nervous hands. Nervous everything. I couldn't even look at Angela. I didn't know that Boone was going to grill her. And why at Independence Hall of all places? The leather chairs in the coach were a lot more comfortable than the rickety antique chairs we were sitting on.

"Did the Secret Service interview you?" Boone asked.

"They came to the loft several times, but they talked to my dad. They didn't ask me anything."

"What do you know about Malak's childhood?" Boone asked.

"Not much," Angela said. "She was born in Lebanon. Her birth parents were killed in an accident and she was adopted by another Lebanese couple. They immigrated to the U.S. when she was a baby."

"What were her parents like?" Boone asked.

"I've never met them," Angela said.

I stopped right in the middle of my shuffle and looked over at her.

"I don't know all the details," Angela continued. "But her parents disowned her when she was eighteen years old. They wanted her to marry someone from Lebanon, but she refused.

She left home and went to work teaching English as a second language. It took her six years to get her law enforcement degree working full-time and going to school at night. The Secret Service hired her right out of college because of her perfect GPA and her language skills. At the time, she was fluent in Lebanese, Farsi, Italian, French, and German."

If Boone was surprised he didn't act like it. "Did she ever say anything about brothers or sisters?" he asked.

"She didn't have any," Angela answered. "Her adopted parents couldn't have children. That's why they adopted her."

"And in all the time Malak was with you she and her parents never had any contact, even by phone?"

Angela shook her head. "Not that I know of. I think when they disowned her, she disowned them."

(My mom didn't get along with her parents either, but they still talked a few times a year and they had visited us in Sausalito a couple of times. They live in North Carolina and Mom planned to see them when the tour headed south.)

"Were you and Malak close?" Boone asked.

"I thought we were," Angela said.

"What do you mean you *thought* you were?" Boone asked.

"Well...I mean..." Angela's eyes started to tear. "We used...to..."

She was back in the produce truck. This time I tried to be more helpful. "What Angela's saying is that if her moth...if Malak...is still alive how could she let Angela and Roger think that she was dead?"

Angela gave me a grateful look.

Boone went over to a side table and got some tissue for her. "I'm really sorry to dredge up these painful memories," he said, taking his seat again. "But it's necessary."

"I'll be fine," Angela said, wiping her eyes.

Boone gave her a couple of seconds, then started in again. "Was Malak different the last couple of years she was with you?"

"She was gone more than usual, which means she was hardly home at all. And when she was home she was often distracted. Sometimes she would get a call in the middle of the night, leave the loft, and be gone for hours. When she'd come back I could tell she was upset, even though she tried not to show it."

"Do you think those calls came from her office?"

Angela thought about this for several seconds, then shook her head. "I don't think so."

"Why?" Boone asked.

"I'm not certain. I'd heard her take dozens of calls from the Secret Service and she never reacted that way. She was all business, unemotional. But she was very different after these calls. They seemed more...I don't know...personal."

"Did your father ever talk to you about Malak's behavior?"

"No. And I doubt that he noticed. When he's writing music—and back then that was almost every waking moment—he lives inside his head and what's going on around him isn't even on his radar."

"The last time you saw Malak what did she say to you?" Boone asked.

"She said that she was going away and wouldn't be home

for awhile."

"Did she seem worried?"

"Not really."

"Did she call you after she left?"

"No," Angela said. "But that wasn't unusual, especially when she was traveling overseas because of the time differences. What's this all about, Boone?"

"I'm not sure yet," he said. He fiddled with the recorder, but I noticed he didn't turn it off. "Let me first explain how you ended up saddled with an old spook. I got a call from a friend of mine, and a friend of your mother's."

I wondered if he was talking about Mr. Potus.

"He got a call from a friend who used to work for the Mossad. They asked what he knew about Malak Tucker's death. He was a little shocked because he didn't know that Malak had been killed."

Not a very close friend, I thought.

"He got the intelligence reports and passed them on to his Mossad friend, but a couple of things didn't seem right to him. He's worked in the intelligence field for years and has a sixth sense about these things. I think the thing that really got his hackles up was the Mossad's interest in her death. They don't ask about things unless they have a reason. Anyway, instead of passing it on to the CIA, FBI, or Homeland Security he asked me to look into it."

"So, no one knows about Eben except you and this guy?" I asked.

Boone nodded. "So far. But eventually one of the other agencies is going to get wind of this and start looking into it.

We want to find out as much as we can before that happens."

"Why?" Angela asked.

"So they don't muck things up before I figure out what's going on," Boone answered. "My original plan was to insert myself into your life by becoming your driver. I wanted to find out what you and your dad knew about Malak's death. I thought it would take me about a week, then I'd get off the coach and disappear into the sunset. Fortunately for you, I found the tracking device, which led me to Eben Lavi, and my plan changed dramatically."

Boone got up and started pacing.

"We've reached an interesting crossroad," he said. "Which way we go from here is up to you." He tightened the rubber band at the end of his braid. "I assume you both know that if you tell your parents about this they'll certainly get rid of me. And I wouldn't be surprised if they pulled the plug on the tour."

Angela and I nodded.

"I wouldn't blame them on either count," Boone said. "The other downside of telling them is that they'll probably go to the Secret Service or another agency." He stopped pacing and looked at us. "The best way for me to protect you and get to the bottom of all this is for us to keep this between ourselves for the time being. So, before I go any further I need your word that what I'm about to tell you will go no further than the three of us."

Angela looked at me.

I shrugged. "You said you wanted to be a secret agent."

"What?" Boone said.

"Never mind," Angela said, her face flushing. "We'll keep it between us."

Boone looked at me.

I held up my right hand. "I'm in."

Boone nodded and resumed pacing. "Now, I'm going to tell you some things about Malak that you didn't know," he said. "In the last two years of her career as a Secret Service agent she uncovered and busted more terrorist cells than any other agent in the world. She was personally responsible for foiling three bombing attempts in the United States and two others overseas. She always seemed to be one step ahead of the terrorists and eventually this got her into trouble."

"Why?" Angela asked.

"Professional jealousy," Boone answered. "You think terrorists are divisive? Just step into the offices of the FBI, Secret Service, or the CIA and the people who work there will *show* you what the word means. Career government workers don't like to be shown up. And Malak showed up just about everyone. She didn't rub her successes in their faces, she wasn't arrogant about it, but she was a maverick."

"What do you mean?" Angela asked.

"Let's just say that she didn't always go through the proper channels. She often operated on her own without the knowledge of her bosses or backup from her fellow agents. People began to wonder where she was getting her information, what her sources were. She refused to tell them. When she disappeared she was being investigated by the CIA, the FBI, and her own Secret Service."

"She never said a thing about this," Angela said.

"She wouldn't have," Boone said. "Not only that, she didn't complain about the scrutiny she was under, or even pay attention to the largely bogus investigations. She just continued to do her job with a single-minded dedication I've never seen in any other agent. And I include myself in this group. Malak was a better agent than I ever was. She was a phenomenon."

"You sound like you knew her," I said.

"Most of what I know about her came from her dossier, but I did meet her once...unofficially. It was years ago. I went to the White House for a briefing when she was on presidential security detail. Looking like I do, you can imagine that the Secret Service paid particular attention to me. Malak patted me down *after* I went through the metal detector to make darn sure I hadn't beaten the machine." He smiled at Angela. "She was a great agent even back then."

Angela returned his smile.

I frowned and said, "You still haven't told us why we're at Independence Hall." I braced myself for another kick from Angela, but it didn't come. I guess she wanted to know why we were there too.

"What do you know about Islamic terrorism?" Boone asked.

I had a feeling that I was about to learn more about it than I wanted.

"I know about 9/11," I said. "I know we invaded Iraq and Afghanistan. I know about Osama bin Laden. I guess that's about it."

Boone turned his attention to Angela. "How about you?"

"Mom talked about the war on terrorism a lot," Angela

said. "I've read several books on it and dozens of articles."

I figured she would one-up me on this subject.

Boone stopped pacing and leaned both hands on the end of the table.

"There are something like one-and-a-half-billion Muslims around the world," he began. "And just like the two-billion-plus Christians, most of these Muslims are wonderful people. Very few Muslims are terrorists, but these days most terrorists are Muslims. And this small group is off its chains. The press talks about terrorists being *radicalized*, but that's not how terrorists see themselves. They think they've been *enlightened*. Terrorists don't think they're bad. They justify their bombings and beheadings and other atrocities on fervent religious beliefs. They say that God is on their side. Christians say that God is on their side. The war we're fighting is a religious war, which is the worst kind of war. Bottom line…regardless of your religious beliefs we can't have people killing innocent citizens."

Boone pointed to my cards. "But the terrorists are holding a pretty high hand. They're smart, organized, well funded, and willing to die for what they believe. They don't have rules, but we do, and they use our rules against us. They know a lot more about our cards than we know about theirs." He paused. "And now they're operating right here, in the United States."

"What do you mean they're operating here?" Angela asked.

"Cells," Boone answered. "Probably dozens of them. And I think they've been here for years…waiting."

"Do you mean sleeper cells?" Angela asked.

"Something like that," Boone answered.

"Wait a second," I said. "What's a sleeper cell?"

"A group of people inserted into the country, legally or illegally, with families, and legitimate jobs," Boone explained. "They live in neighborhoods, their kids go to public schools, they're involved in the community. Their friends, neighbors, and co-workers would never guess in a million years that they're here to destroy the country. On the outside they're living the American Dream. On the inside they're waiting to demolish that dream. One word from their handlers and the nightmare begins."

Boone let this sink in for a moment, then continued, "This is what Malak was concentrating on. One of the bombings she prevented here was a clumsy run-of-the-mill attempt by a well-known terrorist group, but the second and third were elaborate and sophisticated. Had either of these worked it would have been demoralizing for the country." He paused again. "Unfortunately, Malak found the bombs, but she didn't catch the people who planted them."

"I haven't heard about any of these aborted bombings on the news," Angela said.

"That because we're not reporting domestic acts of terrorism unless they're on such a scale that they can't be kept secret," Boone answered.

"Why?" I asked.

"The rationale is that it would scare everyone so badly that it might affect our economy. The other reason is that we don't want to give the terrorists publicity through the media, which is exactly what the terrorists want. The terrorist act is only the fuse. The real damage comes from social and economic repercussions. In our culture that's the real terror."

He came back around the table and retook his seat. "For the past couple of years we've been hearing some disturbing chatter... phone conversations, E-mail, street rumors that this sleeper cell is being run by an anonymous terrorist group. It's said that they've been around longer than nearly all of the other terrorist groups and that they in fact recruit the best and brightest from these other groups. And the most interesting thing is that this organization does not take, or want, credit for their terrorist acts."

"Then why carry them out?" I asked.

"I don't have the answer," Boone said. "But here's my educated guess. Like most Islamic terrorists groups, their goal is to further the religion of fundamental Islam. To do this they don't have to take credit for their acts because they know that some other terrorist group will step up and take the credit for them, which furthers their goal, leaving them undetected and alive to kill again."

"You can't go after a terrorist group that doesn't exist," Angela said.

"Exactly," Boone said. "It's not a sleeper cell. It's a ghost cell."

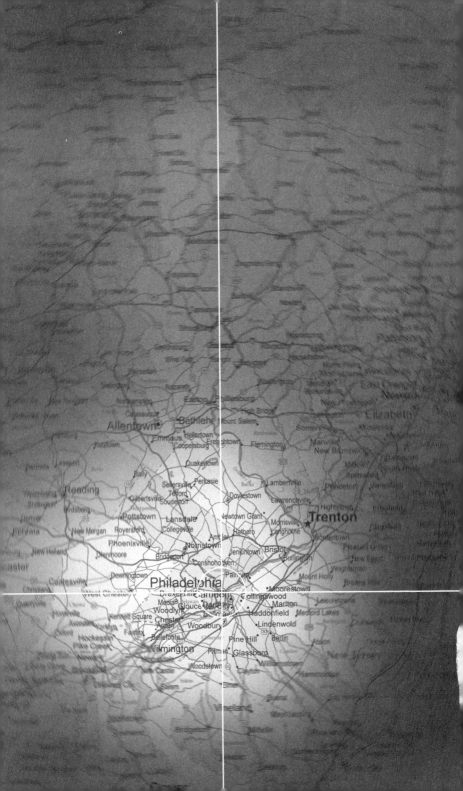

FRIDAY, SEPTEMBER 5 >

Eben walked into his hotel room followed by Carma and Devorah. He dropped his heavy duffle bag on the bed and glanced at the clock on the bed stand. It was just after midnight.

"What's going on?" Devorah asked.

He told them what had happened outside the restaurant.

"Who are they?" Carma said.

"I don't know," Eben said.

"They must be CIA," Devorah said.

"FBI," Carma added. "Homeland Security, National Security Agency, Military Intelligence—"

Eben shook his head. "I don't think so," he said. "Were you able to find out anything about the longhaired man?"

"Virtually nothing," Devorah said. "The security guards at the warehouse are all locals. They hadn't laid eyes on the group before they pulled their coach in. He goes by the name of Tyrone Boone. Do you think he had anything to do with the shakedown in Nevada?"

"I think he had everything to do with it," Eben said. "When they left San Rafael he was not in their coach. They picked him up on the way and I assume it was in the desert when they stopped. Did you get inside the coach?"

"Briefly," Carma said. "But we had two guards with us and they were both hitting on us the whole time."

"We managed to get a couple of bugs in place," Devorah added. "It should be enough."

Eben nodded. "Did you get a photograph of Boone?"

Carma handed him the memory stick from her digital camera. "Several," she said.

Eben took his handheld computer out of his bag and booted it up.

"Where's Ziv?" Devorah asked.

"We split up when we ditched the SUV. He's getting another vehicle. Then he's going to see about finding a spot to watch the warehouse."

"That's not going to be easy," Carma said. "It's mostly industrial around there. I didn't see any good stakeout locations."

"Doesn't really matter," Eben said. "They know we're watching and by now they have a good idea of who we are."

He loaded the photos from the memory stick into the laptop, then ran the images through his database. There were no hits. He then typed in the name Tyrone Boone. Again he drew a blank.

"Do you have any idea where they are?" Carma asked.

Eben clinched his jaw. "No I don't," he said.

He stared at the photo on the screen.

"What do you want us to do?" Devorah asked.

"Relax, but stay close," Eben said. "I'm going to take a shower and get some sleep. They'll have to return to the warehouse eventually. We'll start again when they do."

Carma and Devorah left the room. Eben pulled his toilet kit out of his duffle and started toward the bathroom when something caught his eye. On the nightstand was a guide called, Historic Philadelphia:

The City of Brotherly Love. *On the front page of the guide was a photograph of Independence Hall. He threw his kit on the bed and hurried out of the room. The shower could wait.*

November 30, 2004

"Just a couple more things to do before we leave here," Boone said.

He reached into his pack and pulled out a DVD.

"I'll warn you ahead of time, Angela," he said. "This is not going to be easy to watch." He turned the television on, slipped the DVD in and hit play.

I didn't know what we were looking at until I saw the school group. They looked like they were high school age. It was a surveillance tape of the entrance to Independence Hall. In the upper left-hand corner was a date, November 30, 2004. The same day Malak was killed. I glanced at Angela. She looked a little pale.

"Maybe this isn't a good idea," I said.

"No, I want to see this," Angela insisted.

"This was taken just before closing," Boone explained.

"The Tuesday after Thanksgiving," Angela said quietly.

The guard followed the school group to the door.

Boone paused the DVD and pointed to a boy in the school

group. He had dark hair and looked to be Angela's age or maybe a little older. "Remember him," Boone said and started the tape again.

The school group filed out of the entrance. A couple of minutes later the guard was locking up when a woman rushed in. Malak. She held her badge out and looked like she was shouting.

Boone paused the recording again.

"I want to see this!" Angela said.

"You will," Boone said. "There's no audio, but I have a transcript of what we think was said."

He took a sheet of paper out of his pack and began to read as he restarted the DVD.

Guard: I'm sorry, ma'am, but we're closed.

Malak: Malak Tucker, Secret Service.

Guard: What's this about?

Malak: All you need to know is that this is an emergency and it's a matter of national security. I need to search the building. Now!

Guard: Fine with me. I was about to do my last sweep for stragglers. I'll go with you.

Malak: No, you'll stay right where you are. In about five minutes this building will be flooded with federal badges.

Malak pushed past the dumbfounded guard, through the metal detector, and hurried across the floor out of camera view. The next clip showed her pausing in a short hallway where she drew her automatic pistol and chambered a round. The final clip showed her walking into a large room, automatic out, looking tense. She paused, said something, then the camera shook, and the picture went black.

I continued to stare at the screen even though there was nothing to look at. When I finally tore my eyes away I saw that Angela was staring at the dark screen too.

"So the bomb was here," Angela said.

Boone nodded.

"But you said you thought my mom was still alive."

"I said there was a 50/50 chance she was still alive," Boone repeated. "I have one other clip to show you." He took another DVD out of his pack. "As soon as the guard heard the explosion he called the Secret Service, which was lucky because they were able to keep the incident away from the media. The bomb was intended to take down the entire building, but it misfired. The damage was only in that one room. The Park Service told the press that there had been a minor gas explosion and the Hall would be closed for a few days while they made repairs." He put the DVD into the player.

It was the next day, December 1. Two men in casual clothes stood inside the entrance and checked identification as workers carrying toolboxes, ladders, and other construction gear walked through the doors. The workers wore stocking caps, gloves, and heavy coats as if it were cold outside.

"Don't be fooled by the clothes," Boone said. "They're all federal agents investigating the explosion–Homeland Security, Secret Service, FBI, CIA, the National Security Agency. No local cops were invited to this party."

The picture switched to the room where the explosion had taken place. It was a mess. It looked like an entire wall had come down. A dozen agents were sifting through the rubble piece by piece. In the center of the rubble was an outline of a body in red tape. I looked at Angela. She was staring at the screen, unblinking, with no emotion–at least on the outside. Boone was looking at her too as if he were waiting for her to say something. Five minutes passed on the tape, then ten. The agents continued to sift through the debris dropping bits and pieces into plastic evidence bags. I started to get fidgety. Why was Boone showing this to us? I shuffled my cards, but kept my eyes on the screen.

"There!" Angela said. "Pause it!"

Tears were running down her face.

"What?" I said.

She leaned over to the screen and pointed to one of the workers. "That's my mother," she said.

I couldn't tell if it was a man or woman. The person's back was to the camera and he or she was wearing a stocking cap, bulky coat, and jeans. I looked at Boone. He was staring at Angela with a blank expression.

"Go back a little ways and start it again," Angela said.

Boone rewound it then hit play.

"Look at her right hand," Angela said.

It was gloved, tapping her right thigh.

"So?" I said.

Angela looked at me and bit her lower lip in an exaggerated way.

"It's a tell!" she said with a big smile. "Mom always tapped her right thigh when she was agitated or upset. Nervous hands."

We watched as Malak (or whoever it was) slowly made her way across the room, head down, back always to the camera, but managing it without being obvious or suspicious.

"She's limping," Angela said.

It wasn't pronounced, but I saw it too. The agent was favoring his or her left leg.

The picture switched to the hallway where Malak had un-holstered her automatic the day before. Again, the worker was careful not to show his or her face to the camera, but it appeared totally natural. Three people walked past and none of them gave the worker a second look. The final clip was of the worker striding across the entry room, past the men checking ID, through the front door, and out into the cold.

"Before you ask," Boone said, ejecting the disc, "the body under the rubble was positively identified as Agent Malak Tucker. She was wearing the same clothes she had on the day before. Her badge was in her pocket. Her automatic was a few feet away. As far as the U.S. government is concerned your mother died in an explosion at Independence Hall on November 30 that did not officially happen."

"I don't get it," I said.

"I swear the woman in the DVD was my–" Angela began, but Boone cut her off.

"I have another clip to show you." He popped the second DVD out and slipped in a third.

"This was taken a month ago in Paris."

It was a video of a woman sitting at a table in an outdoor café. She was wearing sunglasses and her hair was short, but she looked remarkably like Angela's mother. She was sitting between two men and she was smiling at one of them as if he'd said something that amused her.

"Where did you get this?" Angela asked quietly.

Boone paused the DVD. "We lifted it from Eben Lavi's computer while he was being detained in Nevada. It was encrypted, but my tech guy is very good. This is fresh intel and we're still putting things together, but this video is a big part of the puzzle. It was taken by a Mossad agent named Aaron Lavi—Eben's younger brother. The man on Malak's right is Salim Kazi. He was loosely connected to Al Qaeda and responsible for at least six terrorist bombings that we know of."

"Was?" I asked.

Boone nodded. "His body was found in Tijuana, Mexico three weeks ago. Before he died he was beaten and tortured. We assume that Eben caught up to him before he crossed the border. I don't know who the young man on Malak's left is." He took out a color photo. It was the same young man from the Paris café, but he had a carefully trimmed beard now. He was by himself.

"This was taken at Fisherman's Wharf in San Francisco two weeks ago," Boone said. "Do you recognize him?"

"It's the guy from the café," I said.

Angela stared at the photo for a long time then said, "He's older now, but it's also the boy you pointed out to us leaving here the day of the explosion."

"That's right," Boone said. "We ran his photo through our facial recognition software. He's an exact match. Now, let's get back to Paris." He hit the play button.

The video continued. Still smiling, Malak turned and looked directly at the camera. Her smile faded and she turned her head away so we could no longer see her face. The two men jumped up from their seats and started across the street. The camera jerked crazily in a blur of sidewalk, sky, and buildings before the picture went black.

"An hour later," Boone said. "Aaron Lavi was found stabbed and bleeding in an alley. He died a few hours later at a hospital, but before he died he managed to pass this video to the Mossad."

By the Numbers

My head was spinning and I'm sure Angela's was too. Boone started stuffing everything back into his pack as if what he had just shown and said explained everything.

Taking the words right out of my mouth, Angela shouted, "What are you saying!"

"We'll do it by the numbers." Boone zipped and buckled his pack. "One: As I told you, the body discovered in the rubble downstairs on November 30, 2004 had the exact DNA as Malak Tucker. In addition to this she was positively identified by no less than three Secret Service agents who knew her well."

"Two: We ran our facial identification software on the woman in the café. A person can change the color of their hair, the color of their eyes, their teeth, their nose…any number of physical characteristics, but they cannot change the shape of their skull or jaw. The woman in the video is an exact match of Malak Tucker. And the young man was the same boy leaving here just before the explosion."

"Three: Eben and his brother had been on the trail of a notorious terrorist for several years. Her name is Anmar, which in Lebanese means leopard. As far as we know the video I just showed you are the first pictures ever taken of her. The Mossad would have run the same facial identification software we ran and they would have come up with exactly one hit. Malak Tucker."

"Four: Days after the video was taken one of the men is found dead on the Mexican border. A couple of days later the second man is caught on camera in San Francisco—the same city where Malak Tucker's surviving husband and daughter live."

Boone paused and took a breath.

"Five: No agency reviewed the crime scene video taken the morning after the explosion here at Independence Hall. And in their defense I don't blame them. Terrorists generally don't reappear at the scene of their crimes. The videos are taken to document the chain of evidence. Since no one was arrested for the crime there was no reason to review the tapes."

He looked at Angela.

"And six: Without any prompting, even though you couldn't see her face, you identified your mother by the…" Boone glanced at me "…tell. That could be a coincidence, but the chances of someone having the same nervous habit in the same building in the same twenty-four-hour period are pretty darn slim."

He let everything he had told us sink in for a moment then said, "Your mother has, or had, an identical twin." He paused again. "And her sister is, or was, a terrorist."

"Was the woman at the café Malak or Anmar?" I asked. "The angel or the leopard?"

"I don't know," Boone answered.

"My mother is not a terrorist," Angela said.

"But she could be posing as a terrorist," Boone said.

"So you think the woman in the video is Angela's mom," I said.

"All I know is that Eben believes the woman in the video is Angela's mother. He thinks that she's changed her name to Anmar." He looked at Angela. "And he thinks she's going to make contact with you. He doesn't know that your mom had a twin sister."

"My mom would have told me if she had a twin sister," Angela said.

"Not if her sister were a terrorist," Boone said. "And I don't think your mother knew herself until a year or two before the explosion at the Hall. Eben doesn't know how or why, but he believes your mother faked her own death, switched sides, changed her name, and dropped off the grid. As a former Secret Service agent she would have the skill, the access, and the intel to wreak terror wherever and whenever she wanted. And for all we know he might be absolutely right.

"The video in Paris set off a terrible chain reaction. Eben's brother Aaron was killed. The threesome fled France and ended up in Mexico. I think Eben caught up with them there and killed Salim Kazi. The other man and your mother—or your aunt—got away. Then one of them shows up in the very city where you and your father live."

"I thought the Mossad was on our side," I said.

"They're on our side," Boone said, "except when it comes to hunting down terrorists." He looked back at Angela. "As I said, Eben thinks Anmar is going to make contact with you, or that she already has, and that's why he's following you. He's going to wait for her to show herself, and if that doesn't work, he's going to grab you and force her hand. In fact, I'm surprised he hasn't already done it."

"But why would my mother switch places with Anmar?" Angela asked.

"That's enough speculation," Boone said. "You know what I know. We have one more thing to do before we go back to the warehouse."

We followed him downstairs and into the room where the bomb had gone off, but you wouldn't have known it. The room looked as pristine as it had in 1752 when it was finished.

Boone began walking the perimeter of the room staring up at the ceiling. "What's he doing?" I asked.

"He's looking for the blind spot," Angela said. "If there

were two people in the room when the bomb went off Anmar was standing in a place where the cameras couldn't see her."

"That's right," Boone said. "There's a blind spot in every room, but they're hard to find without looking at the surveillance monitors. Security cameras have different lenses with different coverage." He pointed up at one of the cameras. "You can't tell from down here what kind of lens is up there. That means that the kid who planted the bomb was *told* where to put it by someone with a lot of intel and training."

"Kid?" I said.

"Remember the kid with the school group," Boone said. "The young man at the Paris café and Fisherman's Wharf. He planted the bomb on November 30. It took the FBI days to figure that out. By then the kid and his family were long gone. They'd only been in Philly for three weeks. They were sent here specifically to blow up this building. And it might have worked if one of the leads hadn't come out of the explosives stashed in his lunch pack. It was detonated remotely somewhere outside the building. Probably by the kid's father or mother, or handler, as soon as they saw him get onto the school bus safely."

"Then what was Anmar doing here?" I asked.

"I don't know," Boone answered. "She might have been trying to defuse the bomb when Malak came in. If that's the case she saved Malak's life because there were enough explosives in that lunch pack to turn this building into dust."

"I don't understand how Anmar got in here without being recorded by at least one of the cameras," Angela said. "The FBI must have gone over the tapes from the hours leading up to this. They'd certainly notice someone who looked just like my mom."

"You're right," Boone said. "Providing the footage had survived, which it didn't." He pointed to a wall. "This is where the bomb was placed. On the other side of this wall was the surveillance recorder closet along with all the videos from that day. If you're a terrorist who doesn't want to be a martyr you want to make sure you're not caught on video. The blast destroyed most of the footage. The vids I showed you in the conference room were just about all that was left. And they were lucky to piece together those fragments." Boone looked at Croc, who was sniffing a wall on the far side of the room. "I need you, Croc."

Without hesitation Croc clicked his way across the room to him. Boone looked up at the cameras one last time, then pointed to the floor. Croc sat down exactly where he had pointed.

"Any more questions?" Boone asked us.

I had a thousand of them, but couldn't figure out which one to ask first.

"So, my mom came here to stop the bomb," Angela said.

"Like I told you I have no idea what her motivation was. All I can tell you is what her movements were. She left San Francisco on the Friday after Thanksgiving. She got to New York very early Saturday morning and checked into a hotel in Manhattan. She was in anti-terrorist task force meetings all day Sunday and most of Monday. She was booked on a flight to Amsterdam Monday afternoon and she was late leaving the meeting. A Secret Service agent drove her to the airport in a government vehicle and had to use the siren and flashers to get her there in time. She checked into her flight, cleared security, and got to the gate about ten minutes before the flight took off. She got a call on her cell. The gate agent told her that she would have to board or the flight would take off without her. She told the agent that she would take a later flight and rushed off. She rented a car and drove to Philly. They found her rental car out front." Boone looked at Croc. "Stay put," he said.

We followed him out of the room, through the hallway, and into the entry area. Brod was sitting at the guard desk in front of a series of blank television screens, reading a newspaper.

"We're about done here," Boone said. "You can turn the cameras back on."

Brod hit several buttons and the screens blinked to life. "Did you find what you're looking for?" he asked.

"We did," Boone said. "And please thank Mr. Little for me."

"I will." Brod looked around. "Where's that dog of yours?"

"Good question," Boone said, looking around as if he didn't know, either. "We should be able to pick him up with the cameras."

There wasn't a sign of an ancient Blue Heeler missing a few teeth.

Boone whistled.

"Oh, there he is," Brod said, pointing to one of the screens.

Croc had left the blind spot and was slowly clicking his way to the guard station.

Taxi

There was a taxi waiting at the curb. Boone must have called for it when he left us in the conference room by ourselves. It was better than the produce truck, but where was his team? Why didn't we just hitch a ride to the warehouse with them?

Boone opened the back door. "I'll see you at the coach."

"You're not coming?" Angela asked.

I peeked inside at the driver and tried to hide my alarm. With all this terrorism talk I wasn't exactly eager to go for a ride with an old man who looked like he grew up next door to Osama bin Laden.

"I have a couple of things to take care of," Boone said. "It's only ten minutes to the warehouse. I'll be there soon."

Angela slid into the back seat like it was no big deal, which meant that I had to slide in like it was no big deal. As we pulled away I looked out the rear window and saw Boone and Croc standing alone in the street light. A cherry-red Range Rover drove up. (Presumably the same one we had been towing.) Boone and Croc climbed inside. The Rover did a U-turn and headed in the opposite direction. I wondered who was driving.

"This whole thing is…well…pretty weird," I said.

Angela stared straight ahead, lost in thought, and didn't respond. I couldn't blame her. Her mother was either a terrorist, or still dead, which was a lot to wrap your mind around. I pulled out my deck of cards, then changed my mind and put them back in my pocket, thinking the shuffling noise might bother her. So, I pulled out a length of cord and practiced some knots.

The driver hadn't said one word to us and I was about to say something to him like, "Do you know where we're going," when a car came out of nowhere and rammed us. Angela screamed. The taxi did a complete three-sixty and might have done a second spin if we hadn't broadsided a telephone pole. The driver, who still hadn't said a word, was bleeding from his head and it looked like half his left ear was missing. The car that slammed into us had stopped fifty feet away. The passenger and driver doors opened and two people got out. Another car drove up on the other side of the taxi and two more people jumped out. All four of them were wearing ski masks and the two who had gotten out of the second car were carrying pistols.

The driver uttered his first word and it wasn't a word that you'd find in a standard dictionary. (I've looked it up.) Angela had noticed the masked people too and was fumbling with her phone. I didn't think the distress signal was going to help us, considering the masked men were now walking toward the taxi, three on one side and one on the other, and would reach us in about ten seconds.

The driver's phone rang. He turned his head and gave us a maniacal grin. "Got the distress signal," he said. "Thanks. Now get down and hang on!"

"You work for Boone?"

I don't think he heard me over the screeching tires as he punched the taxi into reverse. There was a loud thud like it had hit one of the men, but I couldn't see because I was scrunched down in the seat. He slammed the car into drive and the taxi fishtailed down the street.

Emergency

"You okay?" Angela asked.

"Yeah. How about you?"

"I'm fine. Do you think they're following us?"

By the way the streetlights were whizzing past the windows we had to be going a hundred miles an hour. "Yeah," I said. "I think that's a safe bet." I poked my head above the backseat. There was a vehicle about a block behind, but it didn't look like it was gaining. The driver's phone rang. He ignored it. There was a lot of blood on his left shoulder. His phone stopped ringing and mine took over. It was Boone. He asked how we were.

"Angela and I are fine, but the driver hit his head and he's bleeding."

"What happened?"

I told him.

"How far behind are they now?"

I looked out the window again. "Still about a block."

"Too close," Boone said.

I saw another problem out the rear window. "There's a lot of smoke coming out of the back of the taxi," I said.

"Put me on speaker phone so Everett can hear me."

I didn't think that was such a good idea considering how fast *Everett* was driving, but I hit the speaker button and held the phone up to his good ear.

"Are you okay?" Boone shouted.

"Negative," Everett said. "Dizzy, blurred vision, and the engine's RPMs are dropping."

Great. We had a driver who was about ready to pass out and a car that was about to break down.

"I hit one of them," Everett continued. "Maybe two."

That must have been the thud, I thought.

"We're about ten minutes out," Boone said. "There's a hospital up ahead of you. Pull into emergency. They won't move on you with people around. Can you make it that far?"

"I'll try," Everett said.

Angela had taken over my spot at the rear window. "They're gaining," she said.

Our one-block lead had shrunk to half a block and there was even more smoke pouring out of the back of the taxi. All they had to do was catch up, give us a nudge, and they'd have us.

"Keep the line open," Boone said. "I'll stay on until you get there."

Everett didn't look good. He was pale and his head was starting to wobble like he was dozing off. Angela undid her seatbelt and clambered into the front seat.

"Can you drive?" I asked.

"No," Angela answered. "Are you with us, Everett?"

"Barely," he slurred.

I looked through the rear window. The car was now close enough for me to see the silhouettes of the two people sitting in the front seat.

"There's the sign for the hospital," Angela said. "You're going to have to take the next right."

Everett gripped the wheel tighter as if he were struggling to hold himself up. He made the turn, but nearly flipped the taxi in the process. The car came around behind us, but had to slow to make the turn.

Up ahead I saw the red EMERGENCY sign. "Half a block," I told Boone.

"We're going to make it," Angela said.

There was a terrible sound of metal scraping on metal as the engine seized and died, but our momentum kept us moving forward. The car rushed up behind us. I saw the people in the front seat clearly now. They were still wearing their ski masks.

"What do we do?" Angela said.

"As soon as the taxi stops, jump out and run into the hospital," Boone shouted over the speaker.

"They have guns," I reminded him.

"I don't think they'll shoot you," Boone said. "They need you alive."

I didn't like the "don't think" part.

"We're only a few minutes behind you," Boone added.

Everett missed the driveway and jumped the curb. We rolled to a stop on the lawn across from the emergency entrance.

"Gotta go!" I clicked off and stuffed the phone into my pocket.

"Help Everett out of the taxi," Angela said.

Everett was fumbling for the door handle like he couldn't figure out how it worked.

"What are you going to do?" I asked.

"Just help him!" Angela said, getting out of the taxi.

I jumped out the back door.

The chase car screeched to a stop in front of the emergency entrance, blocking our way. The driver and passenger got out. They still had their ski masks pulled over their faces, but they weren't carrying their guns.

"It is over," a man with a foreign accent said.

I jerked Everett's door open and he nearly fell out on top of me. I put his arm over my shoulder and got him to his feet. Angela was standing about ten feet in front of us facing the two men. What was she thinking?

"Get into the hospital!" I shouted. "Run around them! Get help!"

Angela stood her ground. There was an intense look in her eyes, very much like the look I'd seen in the photograph of her mother at the target range.

"Angela, you really need to…"

One of the men lunged for her. Angela dodged, then kicked him in the head. He dropped like a sack of rocks. Before the other man could react, Angela lashed out with another vicious kick. There was a sickening snap as her foot connected with his knee. I don't know who was more surprised, me or the two guys lying on the grass.

"Let's get Everett inside," Angela said, calmly. She put Everett's other arm over her shoulder and we started toward the door.

"How'd you do that?" I asked.

"Nervous feet," Angela said.

"I'll say."

I glanced back at the lawn where Angela's taekwondo demo had taken place. Her victims were helping each other up.

"They're coming," I said.

Everett's knees started to buckle.

"We're almost there," Angela encouraged him. "Just a few more steps."

Everett tried his best but by the time we reached the automatic door we had to drag him over the threshold. The glass door slid closed behind us with a hiss. I was hoping, and I'm sure Boone was too, that the emergency room would be jammed with broken arms, legs, contusions, and bellyaches. Instead, it was completely empty except for the nurse sitting behind the admitting desk. She got up as soon as we stumbled inside and came around the desk pushing a wheelchair.

"What happened?"

Everett looked even worse in the light than he had in the dark taxi.

"Auto accident," Angela said.

"Is this your grandfather?"

Angela nodded.

"Are either of you hurt?"

"We're both fine."

"Have you called your parents?"

"We left them a message on their cells," Angela said. "They're out of town. Granddad was taking care of us. I got a hold of my uncle though. He'll be here soon."

She was lying almost as well as Boone.

"I'm going to take him back to an examination room," the nurse said. "You can wait in the waiting room."

"Can't we go with him?" I asked. I thought it would be safer to stick close to Everett and the doctors and nurses hanging around him.

"I'm sorry," the nurse said. "We only allow patients in the exam rooms. We'll take good care of him and come and get you when he's fixed up." She handed Angela a clipboard and pen. "Just fill out what you can."

That ought to be simple, I thought. The only thing we knew about him was that he was old and that his name was Everett. And that probably wasn't his real name.

The nurse wheeled Everett away.

I looked through the glass door. "They're coming and the one you blew the knee out on is a woman."

"What?" Angela joined me at the door.

The ski masks were off. Eben Lavi was helping a woman with short blond hair across the lawn. She was in obvious pain as she hopped along on one leg.

Angela and I looked for a place to hide, but all the doors were locked except for the waiting room, which didn't have a door. We stepped inside.

Royal Flush

We were the only ones in the waiting room.

"Now would be a good time to pull a rabbit out of your hat," Angela said.

"I don't have a hat," I said. "And if I did I'd try to pull a gun out of it, not a rabbit. You'd better call Boone and tell him we're still in trouble."

I watched the door while Angela made the call. Eben and the women were making their way to the front desk. The nurse came out from the exam room.

"When it rains it pours," she said. "This place was like a morgue until a few minutes ago."

"She fell and hurt her knee," Eben said.

"Looks like you fell too," the nurse said.

Eben touched his swollen face. "I'll be fine," he said.

The nurse retrieved another wheelchair and helped the woman into it. She handed Eben a clipboard. "You'll have to fill out this paperwork. The waiting room's over there."

Eben saw me and gave me an icy grin. As he started toward

the waiting room a door down the hall opened. Two doctors, a man and a woman, in powder-blue scrubs came out. I wanted to run past them through the door before it slammed shut, but I couldn't leave Angela behind.

I stepped in front of them, "Hi," I said. "Do you want to see a cool card trick?"

"What?" the woman asked.

"A card trick," I repeated. "You know, magic."

The man looked at his watch. "I'm not sure we have—"

"I'll tell you what," I said. "If you're not impressed with the trick I'll give you four tickets to the Match concert tonight."

The man laughed. "I just happen to know that the Match concert at the Electric Factory sold out in less than an hour and that you can't get tickets unless you want to pay a couple of hundred bucks a pop from scalpers."

Eben was halfway to the waiting room.

"You can if you're Blaze Munoz's son," I said quickly.

"Right," the man said. "And I'm Elvis Presley."

"It's the truth," I said. "Roger Tucker's daughter, Angela, is here too. A friend of ours bumped his head in an auto accident. They're looking at him inside."

"Do you always solicit complete strangers to watch you do tricks?" the woman asked.

"Nah," I said. "But I just learned a new one and Angela is bored seeing it. I need a fresh audience."

"Why not?" the man said, smiling. "But I'll warn you. I've seen a lot of card tricks and it's going to be hard to impress me."

I didn't care if he was impressed or not. All I needed was

for him and the woman to stick around until Boone showed up.

Eben reached us. "Excuse me," he said. The right side of his face was starting to turn an ugly yellow and it looked like he would have a pretty good shiner before sunrise. He brushed past us and we followed him into the waiting room.

Angela was still on her phone with Boone and she was clearly relieved that I had brought company. "Oh," she said loud enough so everyone could hear. "I think we'll be fine. Q just walked in with a couple of doctors." She looked over at Eben. "There's only one other person in here besides us. He just came in too. Okay. We'll see you soon." She ended the call and walked over to us.

"Are you really Roger Tucker's daughter?" the woman asked.

"Angela," she said.

The man looked at me. "And what's your name?"

"Q," I said.

"I'm Dr. Rask and this is Dr. Wilson."

We shook hands.

Dr. Rask looked at Angela. "Q said that he wanted to show us a card trick and if we weren't impressed he'd give us Match concert tickets."

Angela smiled. "Then I wouldn't count on those tickets," she said. "People are usually impressed with Q's card tricks."

Angela had never seen me do a card trick, but she was right…people are usually impressed. I hoped I had set up everything right and that I could draw it out until Boone got there.

I took my deck out and handed it to Dr. Rask. "Take a look and make sure it's just a regular deck of cards."

He flipped through the cards. "They look okay to me."

"Give them a shuffle."

He sat down at one of the coffee tables and gave the deck several good shuffles.

"I'm going to turn my back," I explained. "Spread the cards out on the table and pick one." I waited several seconds, trying to slow the trick down. "Do you have a card?"

"Yep," Dr. Rask said.

"Good. Show it to everyone." I waited another several seconds before asking if everyone had seen it. They all answered yes, except for Eben, of course, who didn't think he was playing. "Okay," I said. "Put the card back into the pile and give the deck several more shuffles—really mix them up."

When he finished shuffling I turned back around. Eben was sitting in the chair nearest to the entrance watching us. I hoped Boone showed up soon. I didn't think the doctors would hang around for a second trick.

I picked up the deck and held it flat in my palm with my eyes half closed as if I were trying to feel the vibration of the card he'd picked.

"It's a spot card," I said.

"Nice try," Dr. Rask scoffed.

"What's a spot card?" Dr. Wilson asked.

"A high card," Dr. Rask answered. "Ace through ten. Don't tell him. If we gave him that information he'd be able to eliminate the thirty-two low cards."

I smiled. Dr. Rask knew a little something about cards.

"Oh look," I said, pointing to the deck in my hand. The edge of one card in the middle was sticking out a little farther than the others. (This had been accomplished during his definition of a spot card).

"That might be your card," I continued. "But let's not look at it yet. Instead, I want you to look at the card in your pocket."

"I don't have a card in my pocket," Dr. Rask said.

"Back pocket," I said.

He reached into the back pocket of his scrubs and pulled out the ace of hearts. "Interesting," he said. "But this isn't the card I picked."

"I know," I said. "But if you were to draw another card what would you like it to be?"

"If I were playing five-card draw," Dr. Rask answered, "I'd want to draw a second ace."

"I have something a lot higher than a pair of aces in mind." I looked at Dr. Wilson. "Why don't you check in your back pocket?"

She pulled the king of hearts out of her pocket and held it up. "Pretty amazing," she said.

I looked at Angela. "I think you'll find the queen of hearts in your pocket."

Angela checked several pockets before finding it and pulling it out, grinning.

"And this is…" I pointed to the card sticking of the deck. "Go ahead and take it out, Dr. Rask."

He eased it out of the deck and turned it over.

"Jack of hearts," Dr. Rask said. "We almost have a royal

flush. But none of these is the card I pulled out of the deck."

I was just about finished. Where was Boone?

"I don't know what went wrong," I said, acting shocked. "Check the deck and see if your card's there."

Dr. Rask went through the deck card by card, slowly and thoroughly, for which I was very grateful. By the time he got to the end he was chuckling. "That's pretty good," he said. "It's not there."

"Where is it?" Dr. Wilson asked.

I looked over at Eben Lavi. He was still watching us, but then suddenly turned his bruised head toward the waiting room entrance.

"Uncle Boone!" Angela said.

Boone and another man had appeared in the doorway.

"How y'all doin'?" Boone asked in his old twang, stepping into the room.

He was followed by a man half his age and twice his girth, with shaggy black hair, who looked like a professional wrestler. He had his right hand buried in his coat pocket and his unblinking eyes fixed on Eben Lavi, who now had his right hand in his coat pocket.

"I checked on Everett," Boone continued. "He's gonna be fine. I'll get you kids back to the coach. Uly here will keep an eye on things at the hospital."

"Your nephew was just showing us a card tick," Dr. Rask said. "I don't think he's quite done. We're one card shy of a very clever..." he paused and smiled at me, "and *impressive* royal flush."

I was tempted to say forget it, the trick didn't work, and

get the heck out of there. But I couldn't make myself do that. I had to play it all the way to the end. I looked over at Eben again.

"Sir?" I said. "Can you reach into your left pocket?"

Eben stared at me. "Why?"

"Magic," I said. "All of us have a high heart, but there's one missing."

Very slowly without taking his right hand out of his pocket, or his eyes off Uly, Eben reached into his left pocket. He pulled out a card and held it up.

"Ten of hearts," Dr. Rask said, shaking his head. "That's my card."

"I guess we don't get those tickets to the Match concert," Dr. Wilson said. "But it was worth it."

I started retrieving the royal flush from them. "You'll get your tickets," I said, glancing at Eben. "You saved us...uh...or at least Angela from having to see the trick again. I'll leave the tickets under your names at will call at the Electric Factory."

"We really appreciate that," Dr. Rask said.

Eben slipped the ten of hearts back into his pocket. I let him keep it.

Damage

"Maybe bringing you two into this wasn't such a good idea," Boone said.

That's an understatement, I thought. We were sitting in the back of the Range Rover heading to the warehouse. The woman driving our Range Rover was named Vanessa. She looked like my grandmother and was the same woman who had pulled the door closed on the produce truck, which they had *borrowed* and had returned according to Vanessa. I assumed they had *borrowed* the taxi too, but it was not going to be returned. The guy sitting next to Vanessa was Felix. He was middle-aged and even bigger than Uly. He looked like he could pick up the Range Rover with one hand.

"We were in this a long time before you showed up," Angela said. "At least my father and I were. If you hadn't come along we wouldn't have been ready for Eben."

"I still should have known he'd figure out where we were. If Eben hadn't gotten his head cracked in the car wreck he would have grabbed you."

Boone's intel was flawed. "His head wasn't cracked in the car wreck," I said. "It was cracked with Angela's foot along with his partner's knee."

This got everyone's attention. Vanessa looked at Angela through the rearview mirror. Felix turned around. And Boone stared at her with his mouth open in surprise.

"It was no big deal," Angela said, looking down at her lap. "If Q hadn't lured the two doctors into the waiting room with the card trick Eben would have gotten us. All I did was slow him down outside. Q stopped him."

Now they all turned their attention to me. I looked out the window. "It was just a trick," I said.

Boone started laughing and was soon joined by Vanessa and Felix.

"What's so funny?" Angela asked.

"I can just imagine Eben and his crew's shock at being overwhelmed and outmaneuvered by two kids," Boone said, still laughing. "I guarantee that the official version they give to their bosses will be very different than what actually happened at the hospital."

"What happened to the other two?" I asked.

"Ziv has a broken ankle," Felix said. "He'll be out of commission for awhile. The woman with him dislocated her shoulder. She'll be back..." Felix looked out at his side view mirror. "In fact, I think she's behind us right now."

"I see her," Vanessa said. "She's been behind us since we left the hospital. She should be pretty easy to shake, driving one-armed. And that car she's driving is on its last legs."

I turned to look. The same car that had smashed into us

was half a block behind us. One headlight was out. The other headlight was pointing up at the sky.

"Don't bother trying to lose her," Boone said. "We're almost at the warehouse. Once she figures we're settled in for the night she'll back off and they'll regroup."

"Why don't we just call the police and have them picked up?" I asked.

"Because they have diplomatic immunity," Boone said. "A get-out-of-jail-free card. The local police have no authority over them. What we did in Nevada by detaining them was technically illegal. They're not going to let us get away with that a second time. Besides, they haven't done anything wrong…at least anything we can prove. And they might be able to turn the whole thing around on us."

"What do you mean?" Angela asked.

"Everett could be arrested for hit-and-run and car theft. By attacking Eben and the woman you could be arrested for assault. As U.S. citizens we don't have immunity. I think Eben would be happy for us to call in the police."

Boone's phone rang. He listened for a moment then clicked off.

"Everett will be fine," he said. "Mild concussion. They've stitched up his ear, but they want him to spend the night in the hospital for observation. Uly will stay with him."

"What about the woman with Eben?" Vanessa asked.

"She just limped out of the hospital with Eben." Boone grinned. "Apparently they couldn't get their car started and had to call a cab."

Felix turned around and smiled. "Yeah," he said. "I did

a little work on their engine. They'll be spending some of tomorrow getting new wheels. Did Uly get a chance to talk with Eben?"

"Yes," Boone said. "He told Eben to back off."

"What did Eben say?" Vanessa asked.

"Nothing," Boone answered. "He just smiled."

"That's not good," Vanessa said.

I counted off the team members: Boone, Vanessa, Felix, Uly, Everett, our parents' new PAs... "Anyone on our team not accounted for?" I asked.

"That would be Ray," Boone said. "He's our tech guy."

"He's sitting in his intellimobile," Felix said. "He doesn't get outside much."

I was too tired to ask what an intellimobile was. Now that we were safe (at least I hoped we were safe) I felt completely spent. All I wanted to do was to climb into my berth and sleep.

Vanessa brought the Range Rover to a stop in front of the warehouse.

"I'll be in touch," Boone told Felix and Vanessa.

We got out. The woman in the wrecked car pulled up to the curb across the street and parked. Boone nodded at her and we walked into the warehouse.

Bugged

As soon as we got inside the coach I climbed into my berth and Googled *terrorism* on my laptop. I came up with nearly 50 million hits. Trying to narrow it down a little I typed in *Islamic terrorism.* That was much better...there were only about a million hits! I got through about one-eighth of the first Web site before I fell into a comatose sleep.

When I woke up (starving) I wondered if everything that happened the day before had actually happened. Apparently it had, because Boone, Vanessa, and a third guy I hadn't met were sitting around the dining room table talking quietly when I shuffled into the kitchen.

"How did you sleep?" Boone asked.

"Not too bad," I said. "Considering the Israeli Mossad tried to kill me last night."

I opened the fridge.

"There's nothing to eat in there," Vanessa said. "I already looked."

I took out a plastic container of what looked like cauliflower and shook it. "Did you try these?"

"I don't even know what those are," Vanessa said.

I poured a bowl of cereal. At the sound of dry, tasteless flakes hitting the crockery, Croc jumped out of the passenger seat. I poured him his own bowl and joined the geriatric ex-spies.

"You must be Ray," I said to the spy I hadn't met.

He gave me a nod and shook my hand. "X-Ray," he said. "But you can call me X for short."

"X is our wizard," Boone explained.

"We call him X-Ray because he has the ability to see through solid walls, hack into any computer, pick up any conversation," Vanessa added.

It was hard to tell how tall he was because he was sitting, but X couldn't have been an inch over five feet and a hundred and thirty pounds. He was as old as Boone with short white hair, a pencil-thin mustache, and the thickest eyeglasses I've ever seen. When he looked at me his brown eyeballs appeared to be staring through twin magnifying glasses.

"Vanessa means that I'm the resident geek," X said. "In other words, I'm the guy who keeps the SOS from getting themselves murdered or arrested on a daily basis."

"That's the name of your team," I said. "Save our souls?"

Vanessa shook her gray-haired head. "It stands for *Some Old Spooks*," she said.

With the exception of Felix and Uly who were younger (but not spring chickens), some very old spooks, I thought.

"After 9/11," Boone said, "I called in some intel to the FBI and overheard the agent on the phone say to someone else: 'Some old spook is on the line and you won't believe what he thinks. These washed-up nut cases are coming out of the woodwork.' Needless to say they ignored my information." Boone shook his head. "They should have listened."

"I made a similar call," Vanessa said.

"I got brushed off too," X added.

Boone continued. "About a year later the FBI realized their mistake. They called me back and offered me a contract to look into something for them. They wanted to know the name of my organization. SOS seemed as good a name as any."

"Where's Eben and *his* organization this morning?" I asked.

"Ziv, Eben's driver, is still in the hospital," X said. "Rumor has it he's headed home to Tel Aviv and that he's going to have a limp for the foreseeable future. Carma is in her hotel room nursing her sore knee. Devorah, Eben's other cohort with the dislocated shoulder, is sitting outside in the smashed rental car with a telephoto lens pointed at the warehouse. She has to be getting tired by now. She's been there all night."

"And Eben?" I asked.

X shrugged. "We have no idea where he is. All we know is that he's probably pretty ticked off about getting his butt kicked by a little girl and outfoxed by an amateur magician last night. I don't suppose you'd show me how you pulled off that royal flush trick?"

"Sorry," I said. "Top secret."

X grinned. "You and I, Q, are going to get along just fine."

"What about Everett?" I asked. "Is he okay?"

"Everett wasn't normal before he hit his head," X answered. "But yes, he'll be fine. Except for a headache, a mangled ear, and a bad attitude—which is nothing new for Everett—he's his old irascible self. He checked himself out of the hospital two hours ago...meaning he walked out the front door without telling them. He's keeping an eye on Carma's hotel. Uly is trying to find Eben, but so far he hasn't had any luck, which is not good. We'll be okay though. Our reinforcements are here. Uly will bring them up to speed, and put them in place."

"You brought more people in?"

"A lot more," Boone said. "After last night we realized that we needed to harden our security. We've brought in some specialists." He slid a pad of paper across the table. Scrawled on the front page was: The coach is bugged. They're listening to every word we say. Follow my lead.

I looked around (rather stupidly) thinking that I might be able to see the bugs and wondering if I'd already said something stupid.

Why didn't you tell me! I wrote back.

Boone wrote: So you would speak naturally and not give us away.

I wrote: How did they get into the coach to plant the bugs?

Boone wrote: Bribed or charmed a security guard. Or one of the guards is a sympathizer. Or a Mossad agent. Ask me how Angela is doing?

"How's Angela doing?" I asked as naturally as I could.

"She's not feeling too well," Boone said. "Which is understandable after last night. She's distraught. We finally got her to sleep about an hour ago. We had to give her a sedative."

I knew this wasn't true because the curtain across Angela's berth had been wide open when I climbed down and she wasn't there. She wasn't in our parents' room either because I'd looked before I came into the kitchen. Since Felix was the only person Boone hadn't mentioned I assumed they had moved her during the night and he was guarding her. Although, after watching Angela in action she seemed more than capable of taking care of herself.

I wrote: Where is she?

Boone wrote: Safe.

I didn't like this vague, evasive answer, but I let it go and wrote: Why don't you just get rid of the bugs?

Boone wrote: Because this way we can feed Eben information we want him to hear. Ask me what I think Eben will do?

I did.

"He will either bring in more people," Boone explained. "Or he'll try to rectify the situation himself with his present team—damaged as they are. He now knows that you and Angela can extradite yourselves from a dicey situation. Next time he's going to be more careful and come in much harder."

"Smashing into our taxi, a high speed chase through downtown Philadelphia, and a fistfight at a hospital wasn't aggressive?" I blurted out.

"I think that was Carma or Devorah," X said. "After we figured out who they were I accessed their dossiers. They're notoriously impulsive and violent. If it had been one of them that spotted Malak in Paris instead of Eben's brother they would have taken the shot with a gun not a camera and none of us would be sitting here."

Boone gave Ray a frown. Ray shrugged and wrote: We have to keep this real or they'll know we know the coach is infested with listening devices. We need to "worry" them with the intel we have.

Reluctantly Boone said, "Ray's probably right, but it was still a stupid move on their part. You and Angela could have been killed. Where would they be then?" He looked at his watch. "We'd better head over to the Electric Factory."

"Why?" I asked.

"Because your parents have already made their first appearance on national television. If we hurry we might be able to catch their second performance."

In all the terrorist spy stuff I'd completely forgotten about that little detail. "What about—"

Somehow Boone read my mind and interrupted me just in time. "Your parents?" he asked. (Like an idiot I was actually going to ask about Angela and if she was someplace where she could watch *The Today Show*. It was going to take me awhile to get used to double thinking everything that came out of my mouth.)

"Yeah," I said nervously. "Have you talked to them?"

"Early this morning," Boone answered. "I promised that I would find a place for you and Angela to watch the show, although we'll have to get a tape of it for Angela. I don't want to wake her." He pointed to the sofa and held his finger to his lips. "I'll wake Felix up and he'll stay here with Angela."

Croc was alone on the sofa cleaning up after his delicious breakfast. Felix was nowhere to be seen.

Boone got up from the table. "They have a television over at the Electric Factory and they're waiting for us. Also, I think you promised a couple of doctors tickets to the concert tomorrow night."

I was happy to get away from the bugs. I finished my cereal, then went into the bathroom to change. While I was in there I got a long text message from Angela with several things she wanted me to do. It looked like something Buddy T. would write. I wrote her back.

By the time I came out Vanessa and Ray were gone.

No More Secrets

Boone, Croc, and I stepped out of the coach. There were three security guards watching the warehouse—two at the entrance and a third sitting at a desk reading the sports section of the newspaper. They were all overweight and sleepy-looking. None of them looked like they could possibly be Mossad agents or terrorists. In fact, they couldn't have looked more regular. But I guess that was the point. Spooks aren't supposed to look like spooks.

Boone stopped at the desk. "The gal is inside sleepin'," he said. "Felix is with her. Don't go disturbin' her. If Felix needs something he'll come on out and ask."

The guard looked up from his newspaper. "We won't bother them."

"Thanks, partner," Boone said. "By the way, has anyone come by tryin' to get into the warehouse?"

"It's not exactly a secret that you're parked inside here," the guard said. "We had some reporters come by this morning, but they took off when we told them Match was in New York doing *The Today Show*. We didn't tell them the kids had stayed behind. And that reporter or paparazzi woman is still across the street with her camera. We told her that no one was here but you guys, but she's hanging tough. There's nothing we can do about her sitting in her car. It's a free country." He picked up a clipboard and flipped through a few pages. "Yesterday after you left there were a couple of fans who tried to talk their way into the warehouse, but they were turned away."

"What'd they look like?" Boone asked.

The guard shook his head. "It doesn't say in the report and I wasn't here." He nodded at the guards standing at the entrance. "They weren't here either. We had a different crew yesterday."

"We'll be back in a bit," Boone said.

I followed him outside. The so-called paparazzi/reporter was Devorah with the dislocated shoulder. Her smashed car was still parked across the street. She didn't even bother trying to hide. In fact she took a one-handed photo of us.

Boone paused outside the entrance, completely ignoring Devorah, and scanned the street in both directions including the buildings, windows, and the rooftops.

"I think we're clear," he said.

"What do you mean?"

"We'll know in a minute, but I think Devorah has us solo this morning. If she follows us it means that Eben, or someone else, is watching the warehouse waiting to see if Angela comes out. When Ray and Vanessa left the warehouse a few minutes ago on foot, one headed to the right one headed to the left. Divide and conquer. No one followed them. Unless Eben has a lot of people on the ground—and I don't think he does—he can't watch all of us."

Boone started walking toward the Electric Factory.

"Did Devorah and Carma plant the bugs in the coach?" I asked, catching up.

"Probably," Boone said. "Electronic surveillance isn't their specialty, but I'm sure they've been trained to do it. I'm not going to underestimate them…" He glanced back at Devorah's car. She was still inside. "…or Eben, ever again."

"Like they underestimated Angela?" I said.

"Like we all underestimated Angela." Boone looked at me. "We underestimated you too. Getting those doctors to keep you company was a stroke of genius."

I still didn't think the trick was that big a deal, but I flushed a little at the compliment.

"I might as well get this out of the way," Boone said, stopping. "I made a terrible mistake last night. I should have had a cover team on you in case Eben made a move. It was stupid of me. I nearly threw in the towel because of the blunder. I was going to call your parents and tell them what was going on, but Angela and Vanessa talked me out of it. I'm still not sure that was the right decision. If something had happened to you and Angela…" He closed his eyes and shook his head.

"Where did you have this conversation?" I asked.

"In a quiet corner of the warehouse where we couldn't be overheard," Boone answered. "Luckily, Vanessa discovered the bugs inside the coach right after you climbed into your berth or Eben would have gotten an earful."

This explained how I had missed all the action the night

before—not that I would have heard anything in my comatose state. I asked him how Angela and Vanessa talked him out of calling Mom and Roger and spilling his guts.

"Angela brought up again the fact that your parents would quit the tour before it got started," Boone explained. "With an added twist... If they canceled their tour without telling people why, there would be a firestorm of media coverage and speculation that would burn for months. So far no one's paid much attention to Roger's supposedly deceased wife. It wouldn't take long for them to dig up the fact that Malak was a Secret Service agent who died in the line of duty under mysterious circumstances." He started walking again. "If that came out who knows where it would go. Angela said...and I quote: 'If you figured out that my mom had an identical twin, a reporter will figure it out.' I'm not sure she's right. The secret is buried pretty deep, but a tenacious reporter might unearth it. If that happened, Malak, or Anmar—as we hope Malak is calling herself now—would at the very least fall under a veil of suspicion among her own people. Terrorists are even more paranoid than spooks."

Angela had put together a pretty good argument. "What did Vanessa say?"

"She was much more direct," Boone answered. "She said Malak was a dead woman if the twin theory got out. And if the cell got a chance they'd probably make a move on you, Angela, Blaze, and Roger for good measure. Terrorists tend to have scorched-earth sensibilities. I think they'd come after you."

"We could go into the Witness Protection Program," I said.

"It's called the Witness Security Program," Boone corrected. "And I don't think that's a viable option. Your parents are already too well-known to be candidates. They'd have to undergo major plastic surgery. And of course they'd never be able to play music again…publicly, anyway. Roger might be able to compose and write songs under an assumed name, but that could be risky too. His music and lyrics are as distinguishable as his face. Even when a different artist performs his music you know it's a Roger Tucker tune…at least I do. And if I can tell, others can tell, and with the Internet and so forth…" He let the sentence drop.

"So we're stuck with you," I said.

"For the time being," Boone said.

This was as good a lead-in as I was going to get for Angela's To-Do list. "Where's Angela?" I asked again.

"Like I told you," Boone said, "someplace safe."

I stopped walking.

Boone turned around and faced me. "What?"

"That's not good enough," I said.

"Why do you need to know?" he asked.

"Because Angela's my sister," I said. "And if we're going to be in on this thing with you then we deserve to be in on everything. No more secrets."

Boone sighed. "I didn't come into this to recruit you and Angela into SOS," he said irritably. "I came into it to protect you and find out what happened to Malak."

"Believe me," I said. "When we left California I had no desire to be recruited by SOS, but if we're stuck with you Angela and I deserve to know everything that's going on."

Boone sighed then said, "Angela is in a hotel. Felix is with her. Is that good enough for you? Now let's go or we're going to miss your parents' performance."

I shook my head. "No, that's not good enough."

"Well, that's all you're going to get," Boone said and started walking away.

I held my ground. "Last night you said we were either in or out. We're in, but you're not treating us like we're in." I pulled out my phone. "I checked Angela's location before we left the coach. She's at the Comfort Inn on Columbus Boulevard."

Boone stopped. "If you knew that, then why did you ask me?"

"Call it an IQ test," I said. "And you just failed. I want to know what's going on and so does Angela. She sent me a text message. She feels like a prisoner. She wants out of the hotel."

Boone shook his head. "That's not happening. At least until your parents get back to town. If Eben's crew sees her they're going to try to grab her. And for your information, she was totally behind the decision to move to the hotel last night."

Angela hadn't mentioned that in her message. And Boone was right about Eben. He was going to try to grab her the first chance he got. He couldn't grab her if he didn't know where she was. So far I wasn't doing well with Angela's To-Do list.

"What about the secrets?" I asked. "Are we in or out?"

Boone gave me a reluctant nod. "You're in," he said. "But you're going to wish you weren't."

I already wished I wasn't, but I didn't tell Boone that. We

started out again for the Electric Factory.

"I'm not surprised Angela changed her mind about the hotel after some sleep," Boone said. "Felix is not much of a conversationalist. By now he's cleaned his gun at least a dozen times and I'd be shocked if he's said more than ten words since they got to the hotel. He was the only one available to keep an eye on her."

"So, you guys carry guns?" I said.

"It's optional," Boone answered. "But after what happened last night I made it mandatory. I don't like the idea, but if they have guns we have to have guns—not that we're going to use them. Soldiers and cops use guns. Spies use their brains, or at least we try to. Guns are like magnets. They attract each other and all the violence that goes along with having them."

It was hard to imagine Boone, Vanessa, or Ray shooting anyone. But Uly and Felix looked like they might shoot people for sport.

"How did you get Angela out of the warehouse without her being seen?" I asked.

"Through a little window on top of the warehouse," Boone answered. "She and Felix crawled across a board to the next building and slipped out the back. The biggest problem was distracting the security guards while Angela climbed the ladder. Vanessa bet them a hundred dollars that she could stick a knife in a telephone pole from a hundred feet on the first throw. A buck a foot. She won. It also gave us a chance to show Devorah, who watched the whole show from her car, that we aren't as defenseless as we appeared."

I would have liked to have seen that. It would have been

like seeing my grandmother throw a knife.

Boone's phone vibrated and he pulled it out of his pocket. He looked at the screen and said, "Perfect."

"What?" I asked.

"Text message." He looked back toward the warehouse. "Devorah's not following us, which we hope means she's the only resource Eben has on the ground here. And we just got a hit on SOS. Devorah just called Eben and told him who we were."

"How do you know all that?"

"X," Boone answered.

"The intellimobile," I said. The word popped back into my head from the night before.

Boone nodded. "Vanessa wasn't exaggerating when she said X was a wizard. The intellimobile is equipped with the most sophisticated surveillance gear in the world. Some of which our own government doesn't have because X invented it and hasn't shared the technology with them."

"How does it work?"

Boone shrugged. "I have no idea. All I know is that X has some kind of array set up around the Electric Factory and he can monitor virtually everything within a three-mile radius." Boone grinned. "You see, even X has secrets from *me*. It's like your magic tricks. Telling people the secret would ruin the illusion."

"That's not the same thing," I said.

"Maybe not," Boone admitted. "But my point is that I trust X, and he trusts me. We don't need to know everything the other one knows. I'm going to be as straight with you as I can, but eventually you and Angela are going to learn to trust me like the other members of SOS."

Boone pointed back to Devorah's smashed car. "X figured out what Eben is up to by using something called random wiretapping. There is a rather large computer operated by Homeland Security and the National Security Agency. It monitors land and cell phone calls, E-mails, Web sites, blogs, instant messages, and tags certain words and phrases. SOS and Some Old Spooks are two of them, which is another reason we picked the quirky name. When the computer gets a hit it targets the phone. We can pinpoint their location and follow them using their phone signals. We can even get live video of them with satellites. Eben and his crew dump their cell phones every few days and get new ones with new numbers, but we'll be able to keep an eye on them until that happens... with the exception of Ziv. He either doesn't have a cell, which is unlikely, or he doesn't use it much because he hasn't called any of them, nor have they called him. But with a broken ankle we're not too worried about him. Eben picked up a new rental car and parked it at the hospital where Ziv is. He just walked into the hospital carrying a suitcase, presumably packed with Ziv's clothes for his trip back home to Israel."

"If we can tap their phones can't they tap ours?"

"Not without the NSA computer or X's equipment."

"How many people do you have coming in to help?" I asked.

"Zero," Boone answered.

"You're kidding."

"Well," Boone said. "We have Marie and Art who are

looking after Blaze and Roger and they'll be back today. And our pilots…"

"Pilots?"

Boone nodded. "The corporate jet that flew your parents to New York is ours and the pilots work for us. Former military jet jockeys. They help us on the ground in a pinch, but they're not former spooks. That's the entire SOS team. We have no 'specialists.' I just said that to give Eben something else to worry about."

Well now I was worried. I had images of black-clad-flak-vested S.W.A.T. teams shadowing every move we made. I changed the subject so I didn't have to think about the fact that we had no protection except for an old woman who knew how to throw a knife.

"I'm surprised you have a jet," I said. "Mom said you were terrified of flying."

"It's not my favorite mode of travel," Boone admitted. "But sometimes we have to get places fast."

This wasn't on Angela's To-Do list, but it was on mine. I looked down at Croc and asked him how old his almost toothless companion was.

"I don't know exactly," Boone said. "Close to a hundred years I'd guess."

"You mean in dog years," I said.

"I suppose," Boone said.

"And how old are you?"

"Older than Croc," he said.

These weren't exactly forthcoming answers, but I felt I was making some progress.

Slim

The Match semi-truck had arrived and the roadies were unloading the last of the equipment into the Electric Factory. (There were actually two identical Match semi-trucks. The second one with another crew was on its way to the next venue. They would leapfrog like this across the U.S. for the next year. Another expense for Mom and Roger.)

Watching the roadies work was the skinniest man I had ever seen. He was frowning, but when he saw Boone the frown turned into a hideous yellowed nicotine-stained grin. He ran over and wrapped his skeletal arms around Boone like Boone was his long lost father.

"It's wonderful to see you again, Boone!"

"You're a sight fer sore eyes too, Slim," Boone said, slipping into his country bumpkin persona without a hitch.

The nickname Slim was an understatement. The suit he was wearing hung on him like there wasn't an ounce of human flesh beneath the fabric. His Adam's apple was huge, bobbing up and down like he had a golf ball lodged in his throat.

He unhooked himself from Boone and fixed his bulging eyes on me. "And this must be Quest."

I shook his bony hand.

"Q," Boone corrected.

But Slim didn't hear him because he was already talking about Peter Paulsen, aka Speed, aka my real dad. We followed him inside.

"Speed and I go way back," Slim was saying. "And I mean way, *way* back when Blaze was singing with his band. With Speed's guitar licks and Blaze's voice they'd bring the house down, people went into a frenzy. And you look just like your dad…"

Actually, I looked a lot more like my mom than I did my dad.

"…Speed's a twisted wild man!"

Meaning unbalanced and unpredictable, I thought.

"…I haven't heard from Speed in over a year. What's your old man been up to?"

I shrugged. I hadn't seen him since he tried to break into the sailboat at three o'clock in the morning after he heard Mom and Roger were getting married and that their single was racing up the Billboard chart. I'm not sure which enraged him more, the upcoming marriage, or their musical success— and I guess it doesn't matter. He was absolutely crazed that night, attacking the boat with an aluminum baseball bat. Mom called the cops and they hauled him away after jolting him with a stun gun…twice. She went to court that afternoon and got a restraining order against him. He wasn't to come within five hundred feet of us, and this included Roger and Angela.

Somehow his public relations firm was able to keep the incident out of the press—not that the bad press would have hurt him. He'd made a fortune on bad press. Every time he got busted or went into rehab his album sales skyrocketed, which is why Mom left the music business in the first place. "A sick business," she had called it. But I guess she had changed her tune. The success Match was having made Speed look like a wannabe garage band, which was not going to sit well with dear old Dad. Restraining order or not, one of these days, he was going to pay us another visit.

"You missed the first song," Slim said. "But I have it on the DVR." He glanced at his watch (which was so loose it looked like it was going to slip over his hand and hit the ground). "We have twenty minutes or so before the second number. If the second is as good as the first the ticket scalpers are going to make a fortune. The street price for floor tickets are going for over three hundred bucks now."

"I need four floor tickets," I said.

Slim looked at me like I had just asked him to give me the diamond ring he was wearing (loosely) on his left pinkie finger.

"Two under the name of Dr. Rask," I said. "Two for Dr. Wilson."

"Who are these guys?" Slim asked.

"Friends of the family," Boone answered. "Good friends."

"I'll take care of it," Slim said without enthusiasm. "I have the TV set up in my office."

He led us into a large room that was cluttered floor-to-ceiling with music memorabilia. Prominently displayed on

the wall, behind his massive desk, was a large photograph of
Mom on stage singing. Kneeling in front of her was Speed, his
long hair dripping sweat, his calloused fingertips hitting notes
that only he could reach on an electric guitar. But the blurred
little photo next to Mom and Dad was more interesting to me.
It looked like Slim had downloaded it from the Internet and
slapped it into a frame. It was a photo of Roger Tucker at some
kind of award ceremony. He was holding a gold statue looking
like he wanted to be anywhere but where he was. Except for
very small gigs he'd never been a center stage performer, or
"front person," like Mom and Dad. And in the photo he didn't
look like he wanted to be one. Roger wrote the songs and listened to other people perform them. How was he going to do
on live television with millions of people watching him?

Slim hit a button on his phone with his diamond-ringed
pinky, shouted to whoever was on the other end to get tickets
for Dr. Rask and Dr. Wilson, hung up, then looked at Boone.

"What's with this weird X-Ray dude?" he asked.

"What about him?" Boone said.

"He spent half the night here setting up things for the
show, but he wouldn't let any of my tech guys help him and
they're some of the best in the business. He wouldn't even let
them in the room."

"X is a loner," Boone said. "And he's finished his setup.
Your guys are free to do their thing."

"They've been working on the sound system all morning,"
Slim said. "And they said that as far as they can tell your guy
didn't do anything."

"X is subtle," Boone said.

"Yeah?" Slim said. "Well, he might be ripping you off."

"Thanks for the warning," Boone said. "I'll keep an eye on him."

I had to force down a smile. X had probably been setting up surveillance equipment to *keep an eye* on everyone else.

"I got a million things to take care of," Slim said, pointing at the TV. "Make yourself at home. There's Evian in the refrigerator."

I wished the fridge were filled with chocolate shakes rather than French drinking water.

When Slim left I asked Boone what X had been doing in the Electric Factory half the night.

"I didn't ask," he said, pulling a cold bottle of water out of the fridge. "All he said was that he needed to set some things up."

"Trust," I said.

Boone turned around and looked at me. "Now you're getting it." He cracked the lid on the bottle.

"Did you know that *Evian* is naïve spelled backward?" I asked.

Boone laughed. "I didn't know that. Let's see how your parents are doing."

He picked up the remote and rewound the DVR to their first song.

The last person Eben had visited in a hospital had been his brother Aaron. Walking down the antiseptic hallway toward Ziv's room carrying Ziv's suitcase brought back that terrible day.

Eben had been in London when he got the news. He was at the Israeli embassy talking to the Mossad station chief. In his pocket he had a letter of resignation. After nearly twenty years it was time to leave the Institute and find a place where he could forget the things he had seen and done. The terrorists grew stronger and smarter every year. Every time one was killed a hundred more stepped forward to take his place. Eben was tired. He'd lost his passion for the work. The war seemed hopeless and unwinnable.

Of course the station chief had tried to talk him out of leaving, appealing to his sense of duty, his skill, recounting the names of his fallen brethren in the long battle....

Eben listened to the expected argument and pep talk without emotion, undeterred, and was reaching for the letter when the call came.

It had taken him less than four hours to get to the Paris hospital. His beloved little brother died exactly thirty-nine minutes after he arrived at his bedside.

Little brother, Eben thought as he searched for Ziv's room. There was nothing little about Aaron. He had been four inches taller than Eben and outweighed him by fifty pounds—all muscle. Eben was ten years older. He had begged Aaron not to follow in his footsteps by joining the Mossad, but there had never been a chance of that. Eben had been recruited by the Mossad while he was still in the Israeli army and had resisted for a long time before giving in. Aaron, on the other hand, had groomed himself from a young age to join the Mossad. But wanting something did not necessarily make you good at it. Aaron was impulsive and did not always think things through. Eben was constantly lecturing him about this. And in the end this is what got him killed.

They had received some very shaky intelligence that Anmar was in Paris. Eben did not believe the intelligence was credible, but when it came to the leopard they followed up every lead. He would have never sent Aaron over there alone if he thought it might be true.

Surveillance was not Aaron's specialty. When he discovered Anmar he should have called the information in. A surveillance team would have been put on her and the two men at the Paris café. Aaron had made a fatal mistake in Paris, but it was Eben who had sent him there, and because of this, the letter of resignation had remained in his pocket undelivered.

Moments before Aaron died he was able to gather enough strength and breath to tell Eben where he had hidden the video recorder's digital memory stick. Aaron's last words were, "The Leopard...."

Today

All my doubts and worries about how Roger would do in front of millions of people vanished the instant he started singing. It wasn't just his voice, it was his stage presence. The Roger Tucker on *The Today Show* was not the same Roger Tucker in the crummy photo hastily slapped on the wall behind Slim's aircraft carrier-sized desk. Roger's transformation was as complete as Boone's had been the day before.

As soon as he opened his mouth the rowdy crowd was struck dumb as if an archangel from heaven had just landed on the open-air stage. He was singing the chart-topping single, "Rekindled," from the new album. When Mom joined him on the chorus the crowd got even quieter (if that was possible). I'd heard them sing this song a hundred times in the loft, on the sailboat, in the coach, and on the CD, but it had never sounded like this before. It was magical.

I glanced over at Boone and noticed the old spy had tears in his pale eyes. I did too. I was proud of Roger and Mom. I don't think I realized until that moment what a big deal

Match was. And this was just the beginning. I wanted to call
Angela and find out what she thought of the performance, but
I couldn't. She was going to ask me about her To-Do list and
I couldn't talk to her with Boone standing there because most
of the things on the list had To-Do with him.

The song ended and the crowd went wild. They were so
loud that the host, who had stepped onto the stage to interview them, could not be heard above the roar.

"We just witnessed something extraordinary," Boone said.
"I'm certainly glad I didn't call them last night. To have inter-
fered with what we just saw would have been a crime against
humanity." He looked at his watch. "For nearly four minutes
everyone who heard them was on the same plane. There was
no bigotry, no anger, or religious differences. Blaze and Roger
were destined to make music together. The acoustics outside
Rockefeller Center are notoriously bad, yet they just made it
sound like they were performing inside Carnegie Hall."

I guess there was one consistent thing about Tyrone Boone.
He loved music and knew a lot about it.

Roger and Mom had their arms around each other and
big smiles on their faces. They knew they had nailed it. *The
Today Show* host finally got the excited crowd quieted down
enough to be heard.

"Beautiful!" he said. "Outstanding… After this you head
to Philly to kick off your live tour, which I hear is sold out all
across the country."

"First we go to Chicago to appear on *Oprah*," Mom said.
"We've put a cap on ticket prices to keep them affordable.
And we'll add concert dates where we can so everyone gets a

chance to see us."

(Buddy had fought them on the cheap tickets, but Heather Hughes had backed them up and he gave in.)

The host smiled and looked at the camera. "Match will be back with another song in our next hour."

Slim came back into his office. "Time for the second number and if it's as good as the first…" He grabbed the remote and punched the fast forward button.

Eben found Ziv propped up in a hospital bed watching a television suspended from the ceiling. He set the suitcase down, but Ziv did not take his dark eyes off the screen. His gray hair was mussed and his heavy black-framed glasses were askew. Surprised at the old man's reaction to his arrival, or non-reaction, he sat down on the chair next to the bed and stared up at the screen. Blaze Munoz and Roger Tucker were singing.

When they finished the song the crowd erupted into cheers and the host shouted, "Match! Watch for them in a city near you soon!" The host shook Roger's hand and gave Blaze a hug, then the show cut to a commercial for their album Rekindled.

"They're very talented," Ziv said, without taking his eyes off the screen. "I'm going to download their album and put it on my iPod."

Eben was surprised that Ziv knew what an iPod was, and for a second, thought that he had stepped into the wrong room. The hospital was probably filled with sick old men resembling Ziv.

Ziv pointed the remote at the television, turned it off, then turned to Eben, "You look terrible," he said in Hebrew.

"Thanks," Eben said in the same language with a slight smile. He had not stumbled into the wrong room.

"What happened to your eye?"

Eben's eye was black and swollen. "I got into a little scuffle last night."

Ziv chuckled. "With a little girl," he said. "And I heard she took out Carma as well."

Eben didn't comment, but he wondered what had gotten into Ziv. The old man hadn't strung two sentences together since he had joined the mission. Now he was chattering away as if they were old friends.

"Are you on pain medication for your ankle?" Eben asked. That had to be the explanation.

"No I am not," Ziv answered. "I have been broken, stabbed, and shot so many times my pain receptors have given up on me."

Eben wished he could say the same. His head had been throbbing all morning. In addition to his eye, the girl's kick had also cracked one of his molars.

"I just came by to drop off your bag and see how you're doing," Eben said. "Boone and the boy are in the Electric Factory. I think the girl is still in the warehouse. I'm going over to relieve Devorah. She's been there all night in spite of her injured shoulder. Carma is at the hotel tending to her knee. My point is that it's not likely I'll see you before you head back to—"

"Close the door," Ziv said.

"I don't have time for—"

"Close the door," Ziv repeated a little more forcefully.

Ziv's tone both confused and angered him, but Eben closed the door. When he turned around Ziv was staring at him with an intensity he had not seen before, but he recognized the look. It was the same expression his Mossad superiors exhibited when they were upset about a botched mission. But Ziv was just a driver, Eben told himself. A *low level... He stopped himself and took a closer look at Ziv, realizing that he didn't even know Ziv's last name. In fact, he knew virtually nothing about the man he had spent the past two weeks with.*

"Am I in charge of this operation, or are you?" Eben asked.

"I suppose that would depend on who you asked," Ziv said calmly.

"I am asking you," Eben said.

"Then I would have to say that I am in charge..." Ziv paused, "...now."

"You were sent to spy on me?" Eben said with disgust.

"And to evaluate Carma and Devorah's suitability for field work...a task in which they have failed miserably I might add. What did Devorah say about what happened to her last night?"

Eben stared at him for a moment trying to rein in his anger. To his knowledge in the twenty years he'd been with the Institute they had never inserted a team member to keep an eye on him.

"Devorah said that she was clipped in the shoulder when the crazy cab driver threw the car into reverse."

"Did you know that she and Carma had their weapons drawn?" Ziv asked.

Eben and Ziv were in the second car. Devorah and Carma had gotten out first. The street was dark and it was difficult to see with a ski mask pulled over his face.

"No," Eben said, his anger welling up again, but not at Ziv this time. Ziv had tried to replace their automatics that had been stolen in the Nevada desert, but had been unsuccessful so far. "I made it clear to both of them," he continued, tight-lipped, "that there were to be no guns unless we were fired upon. It was supposed to be a simple hit-and-grab operation."

"I was there when you gave the order," Ziv said quietly. "Carma and Devorah disobeyed and made certain you didn't see. Perhaps you should have taken their weapons away."

Eben knew that Ziv was right, but didn't acknowledge the criticism.

"You approached from the right side of the taxi," Ziv continued. "The three of us approached from the left. Do you want to know what happened on our side?"

Eben gave Ziv a curt nod.

"As soon as the driver put the taxi into reverse Devorah raised her automatic and was going to fire into the rear window. She was not clipped by the taxi. I pulled her arm down and dislocated her shoulder. If I hadn't she would have pulled the trigger. One of the children could have been killed, or the driver, who at the time we did not know was working for Tyrone Boone. I was unable to get out of the way fast enough and the rear tire rolled over my foot." Ziv smiled. "As we drove to the hospital last night Devorah was so angry she threatened to kill me with her good arm. Her mind is dislocated and Carma is not far behind."

"I didn't pick them for this assignment," Eben said. "It sounds like you picked them."

"I didn't have much choice," Ziv said. "As you know, with all the terrorist activity around the globe our operatives are spread pretty thin. We're scraping the bottom of the barrel as they say here in America."

"Is that where you came from?" Eben asked angrily.

Not rising to the insult, Ziv said, "I wasn't in the barrel."

"Did they bring you out of retirement? Is that why I've never heard of you?"

Ziv shook his head. "I don't work for the Mossad...officially."

A NOC agent, Eben thought. Like all intelligence agencies the Institute had agents operating without official cover. But he had never heard of a NOC agent being inserted into a team on an active mission, especially as an undercover control officer. Ziv had told him the Institute had pulled him from an assignment in Mexico to be their driver.

"Let's get back to the subject at hand," Ziv said. "I can't imagine that Roger Tucker or his daughter have anything to do with this. And the woman and her son?" he shook his head. "That is even harder to believe."

"It was a long shot from the very beginning," Eben admitted. "We all knew that. But things changed with the appearance of Tyrone Boone. I don't know who he or his people are, but they're players. There's a reason they've attached themselves to this family."

"You can't possibly believe they're terrorists," Ziv said.

"I don't know what they are, but they operate like a cell. I'm going to find out who they are and what their connection is to Anmar."

Ziv sighed. "We don't even know if the video your brother took of the woman is the leopard."

"But we do know that the woman is Malak Tucker, a former Secret Service agent who died at Independence Hall," Eben said. "And that the two men with her in Paris are known terrorists that have been on our hit list for years."

"If Malak had switched sides why would she fake her own death, abandon her family, and disappear from the grid?" Ziv asked. "She would be much more effective working from inside the Secret Service feeding terrorists information than she would working in the field as a terrorist leader."

"What are you saying?" Eben asked.

"That should be obvious," Ziv answered. "I don't believe Malak Tucker is the fabled leopard. You are after the wrong woman."

Eben shook his head.

"It's a fool's errand," Ziv said. "…a wild goose chase. The only reason you were allowed to embark on it was because of your brother and the fact that you wanted to resign. It was thought that if you were allowed to look into this you would eventually come to your senses. That you would rediscover your edge."

"Have you talked to the Institute about this?"

Ziv nodded. "Last night and this morning. In fact, I have been in touch with your handlers every day since this mission started."

"I asked for a team and they give me two homicidal maniacs and an ancient babysitter." Eben reached into his pocket for the letter that he had carried there since the day his brother died. As he pulled it out the ten of hearts fluttered to the floor.

Silence filled the sterile room as the two men stared at the card for nearly half a minute.

Eben broke the impasse by dropping the letter on Ziv's bed sheet. "The next time you report in tell your handlers that I'm out. I'm off the grid."

"I would reconsider, Eben," Ziv said.

"I've been reconsidering my whole life!"

Eben bent down, scooped up the ten of hearts, and left the room without looking back.

Ziv shook his head. The conversation had gone better than he had expected. He pulled the sheet away and swung his legs out of bed. His right ankle was sore—sprained, but not broken. The night before when Devorah dropped him at the hospital it had taken some convincing to talk them into letting him spend the night for such a minor injury.

He stood up and tested the ankle. It would support him. He put his suitcase on the bed, pulled out a set of clothes, and limped into the bathroom.

The man who came out of the bathroom looked and moved like a man twenty years younger. The gray hair was gone and he was completely bald. There were no more glasses and his eyes were blue. The new clothes he wore gave him a look of authority. He looked nothing like Ziv, which was fitting, because Ziv was not his real name.

He removed what he needed from the suitcase and left the room. The nurses and doctors walking in the hallway paid little attention to him.

Ziv stopped at the first trash can and, when no one was looking, quickly rummaged through the contents. When he didn't find what he was looking for he moved on to the second one. It wasn't until he searched the fourth that he found the first item...a discarded cell phone. In the next trash can he found the second thing he was looking for...a set of car keys. The cell phone and the keys' disposal were Eben's first step in disappearing from the grid. All spies had official contingency plans sanctioned and established by their handlers in the event their cover was blown. But smart agents like Eben had secret contingency plans unknown to their superiors in case they were betrayed by those they worked for. False passports, hidden cash, safe houses, elaborate disguises, fabricated histories...everything they needed to reinvent themselves and vanish.

Ziv had reinvented himself many times before and he knew that when this was over he would have to reinvent himself again.

On the way to the car he pulled out his cell phone and dialed a number.

The man who answered said, "Please don't tell me that you want me to drive halfway across the country again."

Ziv laughed, and said, "No, this assignment will be much easier."

Ziv had not driven the SUV from Salt Lake City to Philadelphia as Eben and Tyrone Boone had thought. He had flown from Salt Lake City on a different airline and had arrived in Philadelphia forty-five minutes after Eben. The man on the other end of the cell picked up the SUV at the Salt Lake City airport and had driven it east. Ziv and the man met in Philadelphia and switched places a few minutes before Ziv picked up Eben in front of the dry cleaners.

"Are you back in town?" Ziv asked.

"Yeah. What do you want me to do?"

Ziv told him.

Vanished

Mom and Roger's second performance was as good, if not better, than the first.

During the song Slim stared at the screen like a miser anticipating bags of gold. I caught a glimpse of Buddy standing in the crowd. Behind him were a man and a woman, who looked a lot younger than the other SOS team. I was going to ask Boone if they were Roger and Mom's new PAs/spies, but his phone buzzed. He listened for a few seconds without saying anything, then ended the call.

"Well, Slim," Boone said. "Thanks for the show and the will calls, but we better be goin'."

"What about the tape?" I asked. I was sure Angela had watched Mom and Roger in her hotel room, but I thought we should get one just in case.

"Sure," Slim said, opening a desk drawer. "I'll burn a DVD. It'll only take a few—"

"No rush," Boone said. "We're runnin' a bit behind schedule. We'll come back later and get it."

I didn't know we had a schedule.

"I'll walk you out," Slim offered.

"Don't bother," Boone said. "Heck, I know this old building better than you do."

"That's probably true," Slim said. "I'll catch you guys later." He was reaching for the phone before we left the room.

When we got out of the office I started toward the entrance, but Boone stopped me.

"This way," he said.

"What's going on?"

"I'll tell you in a minute."

Croc and I followed him through the auditorium and past the stage where Mom and Roger's roadies were setting things up. Several of them stopped what they were doing and gawked at Boone almost as if he were the star of the show, not Mom and Roger. He returned their nods and smiles as he led me to a small door. Behind it was a long hallway leading to an exit. Waiting for us in the alley was a windowless, gray, beat-up van with its engine idling. On the roof were several antennas and dishes.

"This is the intellimobile?" I asked. It looked like someone had abandoned it in the alley.

"Never judge a book by its cover," Boone said, sliding the side door open. "Hop in."

I climbed inside. Croc jumped into the front passenger seat next to Vanessa. (I wondered if she had a knife on her.) X was sitting on a chair in the back wearing a Bluetooth headset staring at a row of video monitors. He was so intent on whatever he was doing he didn't seem to notice us climb in or hear Boone close the door. Nor did Everett, who was slumped in the corner with his chin resting on his chest sound asleep. Vanessa stepped on the gas.

"Any sign of her?" Boone asked.

X shook his head without taking his eyes off the monitors.

"Any sign of who?" I asked.

"Angela," Boone said.

"What are you talking about?" I shouted.

"She slipped out of the hotel while your parents were on *The Today Show*," X explained. "She was glued to the TV for the first song and told Felix that she could hardly wait for the second number. When they came back on Felix made the reasonable assumption that it would be a good time to hit the restroom. When he came out Angela was gone with a five-minute head start. She probably didn't listen to one note of your parents' second song."

"What about tracking her with her phone?"

X shook his head. "She disabled it."

"You mean she turned it off," I said.

X shook his head again. "If she had just powered the phone down we could have still tracked her. We have the ability to turn it back on remotely. I tried and it didn't work, which means she popped the battery out or smashed the phone. What worries me is that this isn't something a fifteen-year-old girl would know how to do."

"But Eben knows the routine," Boone said. "And so does his crew."

Boone and X did not know Angela. I told them about the

"spy games" she and her mother used to play. They seemed relieved and a little worried at the same time.

"This isn't a game," X said. "This is the real deal."

"Where's Eben's crew?" Boone asked.

"Devorah is still parked outside the warehouse. Carma is still in her hotel room—before we picked up Everett he bribed a housekeeper to check on her. She's in bed with her bad knee. We put a mini camera outside her door and a signaling device if the door opens." He pointed to a monitor. "This is a live satellite feed of Eben's rental car. He just left the hospital." The screen showed a bird's-eye view of a car driving down the street. "We don't know if Ziv is with him or not, but I assume Eben's solo. Ziv has a one-way ticket to Tel Aviv this afternoon and he's scheduled an airport shuttle to pick him up at the hospital in a couple of hours. But just to make sure he's still there, Uly's on his way to the hospital to check. Unless Eben has more people on the ground than we think, which is a possibility, none of them were anywhere near the hotel when Angela left."

"Any video of her leaving the hotel?" Boone asked.

"Negative. I didn't have any eyes on the hotel. And I checked the various surveillance cameras around the area and none of them picked her up. Felix is on foot trying to find her." X chuckled. "He's pretty ticked off."

"She's probably heading back to the Electric Factory or the warehouse," I said. "Where else would she go?"

"Wherever she's going," X said. "I hope she's smart enough to know that if Eben or Devorah see her they're going to grab her. And pretty quickly Devorah's going to figure out there's no one in the motor coach. Even when people are sleeping there's ambient noise…coughs, breathing…" He glanced over at the sleeping Everett. "…snores. Since we left, the coach has been as quiet as a tomb. And that's not our only problem." He tapped a couple of keys and a woman's face appeared on a monitor. "Guess who was on *The Today Show* watching Match?"

The woman had very short spiky blond hair and was wearing sunglasses even though it was overcast. She was leaning against a barrier. On either side of her were screaming fans. The fan on the right was holding up a sign that read: *Keep on Blaze-in!* The fan on the left had a sign that read: *A Match Made In Heaven.*

"Who is it?" I asked.

"It's either an angel," X said. "Or a leopard."

I stared at the woman on the screen. She didn't look anything like Malak or Anmar. "No way!" I said.

"She's an absolute positive match," X said. "It's Malak or Anmar."

"And she's only a two-hour drive from Philly," Boone added. He glanced at his watch. "She could be an hour away by now. Did you tell Marie and Art?"

"Of course," X said. "But by the time I ran the crowd footage through the recognition software and got the match they were already at the airport getting ready to take off for Chicago."

"No luck with the surveillance cameras around Rockefeller Center?" Boone asked.

X shook his head. "I'm still running some cameras farther

out, but I doubt we're going to get a hit. It usually comes quick or not at all. And Malak and/or Anmar are pros. She knows where the cameras are."

"It doesn't make sense," I said. "She had to know that you have recognition software. There was a huge crowd at the concert. To get that close to the stage she would have had to have arrived at four in the morning. Why would she expose herself like that?"

"Good question," X said. "If Eben had followed your parents to New York I don't think she would have exposed herself like that, which means she knew that Eben stayed behind." He looked at Boone. "She wanted us to see her."

"Why?"

"I don't know," X answered. "But I do know this. If the woman at the concert is Malak she wouldn't leave Angela in Philly on her own with Eben on the loose. She either has people on the ground here keeping an eye on Angela, or she knows we're trying to protect her...or both."

"How could she know that?" I asked.

"Bugs," X answered.

"She put bugs in the coach too?"

"Nope. But she could have tapped into Eben's bugs. Which means she, or someone working with her, has a receiver near the warehouse. If it's another person they could have followed us to the hotel this morning. We should have set up counter-surveillance when we moved Angela to the hotel, but we were concentrating on Eben, not a second group. If she's been watching us she knows where we took Angela."

Boone swore.

The van came to a stop and I was surprised to see that we were back at the warehouse. Vanessa must have been driving in circles. Devorah's wreck was still parked across the street and she was still sitting in the driver's seat.

"You have to give her points for endurance," Vanessa said, shaking her head in admiration. "I bet she hasn't slept, eaten, or peed in twenty-four hours."

Boone looked at me. "This is where you get out."

"What are you going to do?"

He pointed to the monitor. "Vanessa and X are going to catch up with Eben and make sure he's alone in the car. Everett and I are going to give Felix a hand trying to find Angela."

"I'll help you look for Angela," I said.

"Did she tell you she was going to leave the hotel?"

"No."

He fixed those pale blues on me, which I figured were probably pretty good lie detectors after all the years of deceiving people. And the truth was Angela hadn't said anything about ditching Felix. After about a five-second stare he nodded.

"You said you wanted to be on the team," he said.

"Right," I said. "That's why I want to—"

Boone shook his head and pointed out the windshield. "You heard X. Right about now Devorah's beginning to have serious doubts that Angela and Felix are in the coach. The fact that she's still here means that Eben doesn't have Angela...yet. If he had her he'd call her off the warehouse to help him. We need to keep Devorah right where she is. That way we only have to keep an eye on Eben while we look for Angela. And this is where you come in. I need you to use the bugs to convince Devorah that Angela and Felix are in the coach."

"I'm an amateur magician," I said. "Not a mimic. I can't imitate their voices."

"You don't have to," Boone said. "All you have to do is whisper something about how surprised you are that they're still asleep."

"So you want me to talk to myself," I said.

"I'd send Croc with you as a sounding board," Boone said. "But we're going to need him to track Angela."

At that moment Croc was as sound asleep as Everett. His tongue was hanging out, and he was drooling on the passenger armrest. He did not look like a dog that could find anything.

"All right," I said. "I'll do my best."

I glanced at the monitors again. Eben was still driving. The monitor next to it was flashing through surveillance cameras around the city. Malak's (or Anmar's) face was paused on the third monitor.

"How much video is there of her?" I asked.

"Two or three seconds," X said. "You know how it works on *The Today Show*. They pan their cameras across the crowd so the gawkers can wave to their friends. I'm sure there's more video of her that they didn't use on the show. I might try to get a hold of the unused footage, but that could be risky. They're going to ask why I want it and I can't tell them the truth. We don't want a major television network investigating who we are."

"Can I get a copy of those two or three seconds?"

At that point I didn't know why I asked. I had a feeling

that the coach duty was their way of getting me out of their hair. Maybe I wanted to throw another IQ test at them to see what they would say. Or maybe it was because I still couldn't believe the woman was Angela's mom. Something bothered me about it. I wanted to take another look at the video on my laptop.

X looked at Boone.

"It's fine with me," Boone said. "As long as it doesn't take long. We really need to catch up with Eben."

"I'll E-mail it to you while we're driving," X said.

They passed the test.

I slid the door open and started to step out. Boone put his hand on my shoulder and said, "Obviously, if Angela shows up at the warehouse you need to call me immediately."

"Obviously," I said.

Everett raised his head. "Take it easy, kid," he said.

I slid the door closed.

Two Little Angels

Devorah snapped my photo as I headed into the warehouse. I didn't taunt her by smiling or waving. I actually felt a little sorry for her sitting in that car all that time with her bum shoulder and nothing to do but stare at an empty warehouse. Being a spy was nothing like the James Bond novel I'd read. I felt sorry for the security guards too. There was only one standing at the entrance now. He gave me a sleepy nod as I walked past him. The other two guards were at the desk playing cards. I was tempted to ask if I could get in on the game or show them a card trick. But I didn't have the time. I had an important secret mission. I had to go talk to myself.

I unlocked the coach, stepped inside, and quietly closed the door behind me so I didn't wake up anybody in the empty coach. I waited a few seconds, then whispered (feeling ridiculous): "I can't believe they're still asleep." Which I guess completed my assignment. Now what was I going to do?

Eat.

I opened the fridge. The contents had not changed since

the last time I looked. I found a loaf of something called *16 Grain Organically Milled Bread.* (I didn't know there were 16 different kinds of grain on earth.) I pulled a slice out of the bag. It had the texture and weight of a chunk of wood, and from previous experience I knew that's exactly what it would taste like. Way in the back was a jar of almond butter, which had the consistency and taste of wood glue. If I didn't like the combination of the two I decided I'd pass the time constructing a sturdy organic breadbox and give it to Mom as a hint that our food was actually construction material, not food.

"What's to eat?" Angela whispered.

The bread went flying across the kitchen. I'd had just about enough of people sneaking up behind me. I whipped around and was about to shout something obscene, but Angela was holding up a stop sign that read: Bugs! At that moment she was bugging me a lot more than the bugs. At least now Devorah would think Angela was in the coach *because Angela was in the coach!*

"I was about to make a delicious almond butter sandwich," I said. I picked up a slice of bread off the floor with Croc hair stuck all over it. "I'll make you one."

"No thanks," Angela whispered. "And keep your voice down so you don't wake Felix. I'm going to take a shower." She waggled her index finger for me to follow her.

When we got into the bathroom she slid the door closed and turned on the shower.

"X said it was safe to talk in here," she said. "The bugs are under the dashboard, above the dining room table, and in Dad and Blaze's bedroom."

"What are you doing here?" I asked. "How did you get in here without the security guards seeing you?"

"Those guards wouldn't notice the Israeli army storming the warehouse. I came back the same way I left…over the roof and down a ladder. They didn't even glance in my direction. Did you see *The Today Show*?"

"Yeah," I said. "*Both* performances. You skipped out on the second one."

"Weren't they great!"

Angela bit her lower lip. Uh-oh.

"They were great," I agreed. "Especially your dad, but you were supposed to stay in the hotel. Boone's going crazy trying to find you." I pulled out my phone. "I better call and tell him you're here."

Angela bit her lower lip again. Here it comes, I thought.

"Let's wait a bit before we call him," she said.

"Why?" I said. "So Boone and the other old spooks can keel over from heart attacks from worry?"

My phone rang.

"Please!" Angela begged. "Don't answer it."

I looked down at the screen. It wasn't a call, it was the download from X of *The Today Show*. I slipped the phone back into my pocket.

"All right I didn't answer it. Now tell me what's going on."

Another lower lip bite.

"Come on!" I urged her. "Why are you hiding from Boone? Why did you pull your battery out of your cell phone?"

"I just needed some privacy."

I thought she might bite her lower lip off.

"Really? Then why did you come back here? The coach isn't exactly private. It's crawling with bugs."

Angela released her lip and reached into her pocket. She held up a gold chain. Hanging from the chain was a gold angel.

"This," she said.

It looked familiar, but I knew I'd never seen Angela wearing it. I stared at the little angel dancing on the necklace.

"It belonged to your mother," I said.

Angela shook her head and put the necklace around her neck. That's when I remembered where I had seen it before. I took my phone out.

"Who are you calling?" Angela asked.

"No one." I opened X's download and played it. Then I played it again to make sure.

"What are you doing?" Angela tried to get a look at the screen.

I hid the phone from her. "The first thing you asked me to do this morning was to persuade Boone to make us a part of his team." I opened her text message. "Here it is…at the end you said, *Tell him: NO MORE SECRETS!* Seems to me that Boone isn't the only one keeping secrets."

"I'm not keeping any secrets from you," Angela said.

"Well, you're not volunteering information, which is the same thing as keeping a secret. And this is exactly the same thing that you accused Boone of doing."

"Sorry," Angela said.

And she did look sorry so I paused the video and showed

her the picture of the woman with the spiky blond hair. She gasped and grabbed the phone out of my hand.

"Where did you get this?" Her voice was choked with emotion and her eyes started to well with tears.

"X-Ray," I said.

"Boone and the others know?"

"Yeah. X used some kind of facial recognition software to pick her out of the crowd." I pointed to the picture on the BlackBerry. "This woman doesn't look anything like your mother." I reached over and zoomed in on the still. "You saw the necklace."

"I *thought* I saw the necklace," she said. "She was only on camera for a second and the hotel TV wasn't recording so I couldn't replay it." She looked at the little angel hanging around her neck in the mirror. "When I was little Dad wrote a song called 'Two Angels'."

"I know that song," I said. Mom used to play it all the time.

"It was a big hit," Angela continued. "He had these necklaces made for us with the first royalty check. We wore them every day. I took mine off when Mom died. I didn't want to be reminded of her every time I looked in the mirror. And I didn't want to remind Dad either."

Tears streamed down her cheeks. It was bad enough to hear her crying in the dark produce truck, but seeing it up close in the tiny bathroom was worse. I started to leave to give her some privacy.

Angela turned around. "Don't go." She handed my phone back and wiped her face with a towel. "I have a lot more to tell you. But first, why did you ask X to download the video clip?"

Before answering I used the towel to wipe the tears off my phone.

"At first I thought it was a test to see if Boone would let X give it to me with no questions asked," I said. "He did. But then when we got in here and you showed me your necklace I realized why I had really asked. The photo of your mom at the firing range. She was wearing the same necklace, but it only had one charm." I held up the BlackBerry so she could see the screen. "Now there are two."

Angela nodded.

"It's kind of hard to see," I said, "but the second one looks like some kind of cat."

"A crouching leopard," Angela said, then turned off the shower.

Ziv made two calls as he drove Eben's rental. One to Carma. One to Devorah. Neither was happy to hear from him and they were less happy with the news he conveyed. He told them that the mission had been scrapped and was officially over. They were to fly home immediately and report back into the Institute.

Both of them refused.

Carma said, "My orders come from Eben, not his driver," then she hung up.

Devorah asked him where Eben was. When he told her that he didn't know she hung up on him too.

Ziv wasn't surprised. Mossad agents were notoriously stubborn about aborting a mission before it was completed. But Ziv had accomplished his mission. Tyrone Boone would continue to be able to track them. Carma and Devorah would keep their current cell phones until they got in touch with Eben. What Boone didn't know was that Eben's cell phone was sitting on the seat next to him. Eben's cell phone rang. Ziv smiled and let it go to voice mail. It was either Carma or Devorah. He was certain that none of them would call the Institute to confirm his authority to abort the mission for fear that his authority was legitimate. If the Institute confirmed it they would all be on the next flight to Tel Aviv. Unconfirmed, they could remain in the field and claim ignorance if there were questions later—and there were always questions later.

For the time being, Ziv would have three rogue agents on his hands, but he wasn't worried. They were exhausted, injured, confused, and out of communication with each other. He also knew that the phone conversations he'd just had would confuse Tyrone Boone as well.

SOS was very confused.

Uly had just called and said that Ziv was not at the hospital and no one had seen him leave.

"Talked to a nurse," he told Boone. "Sprained ankle, not broken. I found a gray wig and a pair of glasses in the bathroom. Checked the surveillance camera tapes and I think I might have caught him a couple of times in the hallway, but I'm not one hundred percent sure. Whoever it was, was wise to the cameras. Never caught his face. In one of the vids he was pulling something out of a trash can. Couldn't see what it was, but I'll tell you this... If the guy was Ziv he didn't look like Ziv...but he knew exactly what he was doing. He was in complete control."

"How was he dressed?"

Uly told him.

"Oh that's just perfect," Boone said irritably. "Where did he get that?"

"Don't know," Uly said. "I searched his room and found his suitcase and a couple of other interesting items. What do you want me to do?"

"Hook up with Felix and help him search for Angela," Boone answered. "We have to find her before Eben does."

As soon as he ended the call with Uly, Ziv's calls to Carma and Devorah came in. Boone, X, Everett, and Vanessa listened carefully to the brief calls. When the second call ended a look of deep concern was etched into Boone's tired face.

"I guess Ziv isn't out of commission," he said. "Did you get a lock on his phone?"

"Negative," X said. "The ladies weren't on long enough for the computer to snag it. Something's not right about this. We didn't have any trouble pulling up Eben, Carma, and Devorah from the database, but we drew a blank on Ziv. We wrote him off as a low level Mossad functionary...a driver. Either we were wrong about him or they're running some kind of scam. I think there's a good chance we're going to lose all four of them."

"Drop me and Everett off here," Boone said. "The hotel's only a few blocks away." He pointed to the monitor tracking Eben's car. "You need to catch the car before it's dumped. We need to know who's in it."

Boone, Everett, and Croc jumped out of the van. Vanessa peeled out with the sliding door still open.

The E-mail

Angela walked over to our berths and whispered to no one: "Put that book down, Q. We might as well work on our homework while Felix is sleeping. Bring your laptop. We'll work in Mom and Dad's room so we don't wake him."

She was obviously more fluent in "bug talk" than I was. I followed her into the master suite and saw her open her laptop on the bed. This must have been where she was hiding out when I came into the coach.

"I guess we should finish up our Philadelphia section since we'll be leaving here tomorrow," she said. "We'll take turns inputting things onto the Web page." She typed for a minute or two, then turned her laptop around so I could read it...

My mother sent me a TM right after I saw her on the Today Show. It read: Check our E-mail. "Our E-mail" was a Yahoo E-mail account that only she and I knew about. I haven't used, or even thought about it, since I thought she died. In their hurry to get me out of here last night

I forgot my backpack. I couldn't remember the E-mail
address and I didn't think it was a good idea to use my
BB anyway in case Boone or X were monitoring our E-mail
as well as our calls. I came back here to get the E-mail
address from my journal and to use the computer.

I read this over twice and had about two hundred questions like: How does your mother know your phone number?
But instead I typed:

What did the E-mail say?

Angela typed:

Wait outside Independence Hall @ 2:15. Come alone. Do
not tell Boone or SOS. Q can come too if you can't slip
away from SOS without him. Be patient. I'll be watching and someone will make contact when we know it's
safe.

X had been right. Malak or Anmar had somehow tapped
into Eben's bugs. This was the only way that she could have
known about Boone and SOS. And it was clear she wasn't in
this alone.

I typed:

Who is someone?

Angela shrugged.

I typed:

You don't know if the E-mail is from your mom or Anmar!!! What if Anmar took your mother's necklace after the explosion? Why would your mother add the leopard charm to her necklace?

Angela took the computer and typed:

I'm going to be there @ 2:15 to get the answers to those questions and many others. You don't have to come with me, but you can't tell Boone that I was here or where I've gone.

I could tell Boone anything I wanted to and I'd probably be doing Angela a favor by ratting her out, but I typed:

I'm going with you.

Angela looked relieved.

I didn't want to go, but I wanted her to go by herself even less. Also, I thought I might be more successful at talking her out of this if I could actually *talk* to her instead of typing my argument.

Angela typed:

You'll have to leave your BB here. But before you do, find out where everyone is.

I punched the tracking icon and went down the list showing Angela the screen each time I clicked a name. X and Vanessa were together, and by the speeds their icons were moving, they were still in the intellimobile. Uly, Felix, Everett, and Boone were within blocks of each other near the hotel and moving much slower, on foot no doubt, searching for Angela. I wondered if Croc had picked up her scent. I noticed that there were two new names: Blaze and Roger. I clicked their names. It took awhile for their dots to appear on the little screen. They were in Chicago, moving fast. Art and Marie were with them—probably in a limo on their way to Harpo Studios where *Oprah* was taped.

I typed:

Boone is going to call me at some point. If I don't answer he's going to come running.

Angela typed:

By then we'll be long gone.

I just hoped we weren't permanently gone. I typed:

How are we going to get past the guards? Not that they would care if we leave... But they will tell Boone that we left together.

Angela typed:

Boone showed me the back door to the coach last night...
And I don't know about you, but I could use a cheeseburger. Maybe we'll find some horribly unhealthy food
on the way to Independence Hall.

I tossed my BlackBerry on the bed and followed her into
the kitchen. She stuffed a roll of paper towels into her backpack (I didn't ask why), slipped the pack over her shoulders,
then flipped up a sofa cushion. Underneath was a hatch that
led to a storage compartment beneath the coach, which just
happened to be on the opposite side of where the guards were
stationed. I had no doubt that Boone had parked the coach
this way intentionally thinking that we might have to use the
"back door."

Quietly, we eased ourselves through the hatch. We peeked
around the rear of the coach at the guards. All three of them
were now sitting at the desk playing cards.

Up and Away

We crept along the wall trying to stay in the shadows and not trip over anything. There was a ladder attached to the wall in the corner (a very high, unstable ladder that did not look like it would support a squirrel). At the very top was an open window and a row of cooing pigeons perched on the rafters above it.

Angela started up the ladder like a ninja. I didn't think it would hold both of us at the same time. While I waited I watched the guards. They continued to play cards.

I looked up. Angela had already scrambled her way to the top and through the window. Halfway up I had to stop to catch my breath (and scrape pigeon poop off my hands). I hadn't noticed Angela stopping to catch her breath (or wipe her hands). This meant she could not only beat me up if she wanted to, she also had better endurance than I did (and more tolerance for revolting slime). I squeezed through the window onto the flat, tar roof wheezing. Angela handed me a handful of paper towels, which explained why she had put them in her pack.

"Sick, huh?" she said with a grin.

"Yeah." I wiped my hands, but not much of the stuff came off.

As I followed her across the roof to the far end of the warehouse I glanced over the edge and noticed something was missing. Devorah's car was still parked across the street, but she was no longer in it.

"Problem," I said.

Angela backtracked. She looked down at the car, then up and down the street. "I don't like it," she said.

"Me either," I agreed. "It means Devorah could be any-where, including waiting for us outside the back door of the next building. Are you sure no one saw you come back here?"

"I don't think so," she said.

I almost spilled my guts about X's setup around the Electric Factory, but stopped myself. Why shouldn't I have a secret too? Everyone else was withholding information. How had Boone put it? ...*X has some kind of array set up around the Electric Factory and he can monitor virtually everything within a three-mile radius.* I should have asked what an "array" was. Whatever it was it hadn't picked up Angela sneaking back into the ware-house. I just hoped it caught us leaving the warehouse.

Croc had picked up Angela's scent within minutes of Boone and Everett's arrival at the hotel. They followed him as he sniffed along the sidewalk for two blocks, then the Blue Heeler/Border Collie came to a sudden stop and looked up at them. Boone knew the look. The scent trail had ended. Angela had gotten into a car.

Everett examined the ground. "I don't see any skid marks…no sign of a struggle. It couldn't have taken her more than five minutes to get here. At that point we had all of Eben's team under surveillance, except for Ziv." He looked up and nodded at the sign above them. "Bus stop."

"Get the bus schedule and route," Boone said.

While Everett accessed the schedule on his BlackBerry, Boone called Uly and Felix and told them to get the Range Rover.

"I have the route," Everett said.

"We'll go to every stop until Croc picks up Angela's scent. She had to get off the bus somewhere."

Boone's phone rang. It was Blaze. He let it go to voice mail. As soon as the ringing stopped it rang again. It was Roger. He let that call go to voice mail as well. He wasn't going to talk to either one of them until he knew what was going on. He was about to check in with

Q when the intellimobile pulled up.

"This can't be good," he said to Everett.

Uly and Felix pulled up behind in the Range Rover just as the van door slid open. A glassless X squinted out at them. "I got sucker-punched," he said. "Or more accurately…sucker-choked."

Vanessa was sitting in the driver's seat, repairing X's broken glasses with duct tape. X could not see beyond his nose without them.

"This has turned into a really lousy day," Boone said. He called Q and got his voice mail. He looked at the others. "And I think it just got worse."

He told Uly, Everett, and Felix to take Croc and follow the bus. "We'll head over to the warehouse and find out why Q isn't answering his phone. I'll call you as soon as I know anything."

The Range Rover drove off and Boone climbed into the van.

Vanessa handed the twisted, but usable, glasses to X. As soon as he had them balanced on his nose he started fiddling with the electronics. Vanessa started toward the warehouse.

"Okay," Boone said. "What happened?"

"Eben, or whoever was driving the car pulled into a covered parking garage," Vanessa began. "We didn't have enough clearance because of the dish on top. I went in on foot to see what I could find out." She looked back at X.

He stopped his fiddling and picked up the story. "While Vanessa was inside I started scanning through the surveillance cameras. Carma was still in her room. Nothing on the mini-cam, and the alarm Everett put on her door had not tripped, so nobody had come or gone. She's on the third floor…no balcony, no fire escape, no way in or out except through the door.

"I switched to Devorah next. Got lucky and caught her getting

out of the car. I started tracking her with the camera array. As I was watching her I heard the door slide open behind me. I figured it was Vanessa. Devorah was in a hurry so I didn't turn around. Thought I might lose her. Big mistake. The next thing I know there's a large forearm expertly wrapped around my neck. I was out within seconds." He gave Vanessa a dirty look. "Then Vanessa was slapping me awake."

"Okay, okay," she said. "I'm the one who broke your glasses. But I also fixed them."

"Kind of," X said, readjusting the glasses. "Anyway, I don't know how long I was out. It couldn't have been more than a couple of minutes. But in that time whoever took me out incapacitated all of our surveillance. We're completely offline."

"Are you saying that we don't know where any of them are right now?" Boone asked.

"With the possible exception of Carma, that's exactly what I'm saying," X answered. "We're blind."

Boone called Everett. "I need you to get over to Carma's hotel and see if Devorah shows up there… The cameras are out… Yes all of them… I'll explain later." He ended the call and looked at X. "Can the equipment be repaired?"

"Here's the weird thing," X answered. "First, whoever did this could just as easily have put a silenced bullet into my noggin. And I'm going to thank him for not doing that if I ever get a chance to meet him. And second, if they really wanted to take out our surveillance they could have executed the computers the same way, a couple of bullets in the hard drives and we would have been down for days. Instead, they downloaded a nasty little virus into the computers that turned the data into a platter of scrambled eggs."

X pointed to the computers. "I designed this system to be virtually impregnable. There are only a handful of people that might…and I emphasize might…be able to hack into it. And I know all of them personally, or at least I thought I did. If the information in their dossiers is accurate…and I believe it is…there's no way Eben, Carma, or Devorah could have done this. And besides, they would have taken the equipment out permanently. It's going to take awhile, but I can fix this."

"Are you saying it was the mysterious Ziv?" Boone asked.

"It could have been," X answered. "But on the way over here I remembered something from Malak's dossier. She spent six months over at NSA being trained by their computer geeks. I know the guy who trained her. I called him, thinking he wouldn't remember her from Adam. He trains hundreds of agents a year and has a terrible memory for names. When I asked if he remembered a Secret Service agent named Malak Tucker he went crazy saying that she was the most brilliant student he'd ever had. He offered her a position working with him. She turned him down, saying that she wanted to stay in the field."

Boone looked at his watch. "I don't think she could have gotten here from New York in time."

"I agree," X said. "But she could have concocted the virus, put it on a flash drive, and had whoever choked me inject it into our system."

Corndogs and Tastykakes

After about a mile of walking I gave up on Vanessa screeching the van to a halt and Boone jumping out to save us.

Angela walked away from Independence Hall, then doubled back, stopping at a convenience store (where I bought two stale corndogs, a really good Tastykake cupcake, and a Pepsi), a restaurant (we didn't even sit down), and a beauty salon (where she made a hair appointment for the following week. She neglected to mention the fact that she wouldn't be in Philly the following week). After leaving the salon she doubled back again, stopping at a department store, where she bought a Philadelphia Eagles cap and a pair of sunglasses.

"How many pairs of sunglasses do you own?" I asked as we left the store.

"I have no idea." She threw the bag away and handed the sunglasses and cap to me.

"I don't wear sunglasses or hats," I said. "But thanks anyway."

"Just put them on."

I did (reluctantly) and glanced at my reflection as we passed a window. The cap and sunglasses weren't much of a disguise, but to my surprise I kind of liked the way I looked.

Angela popped into yet another business—this time a huge discount shoe store. At this rate we would never get to Independence Hall to meet the angel or the leopard. I caught up with her in the sneaker rack, which was about two blocks long. She was peeking through a gap in the shelves at the front door.

"What are you doing?" I asked. "What are we doing?"

"Making sure no one's following us," Angela answered without taking her eyes off the door.

"If Eben and his crew had seen us," I pointed out. "They would have grabbed us already. If the SOS team had seen us *they* would have grabbed us. They have no idea that we're on our way to see your mom. What we're doing is ridiculous."

Angela looked at me. "I'm using standard counter-surveillance tactics."

She couldn't see me rolling my eyes under my shades and I wondered if she was doing the eye-roll under her shades too…and how many times she had done it since she became my sister.

"Look," I said. "Your mother (or the most notorious terrorist on earth, I thought) told us to come alone. We came alone. It's not our fault if someone is following us—and I doubt anybody is. We're exposing ourselves to hundreds of people by running around back and forth. If we had walked straight to Independence Hall less than a dozen people would have seen us. If I saw two people acting like we've been acting I'd follow them just out of curiosity."

Angela's sunglasses stared at my sunglasses for a second, then she smiled. "You might be right, but you wouldn't have gotten those two corndogs."

I returned the smile. "That was the only counter-surveillance tactic that made any sense. Let's just stroll straight over to Independence Hall and see if the woman is an angel or a leopard."

The security guards jumped up from the desk as Boone and Vanessa rushed into the warehouse. X had stayed behind in the van desperately trying to concoct an antidote to the virus infecting his impregnable surveillance system.

"Just taking a little break here," one of the guards said guiltily.

Boone eyed the playing cards on the table. "I see that," he said. "Be nice if y'all could take your breaks separately though, if you get my drift."

They did. Two of the guards hurried over and took up positions on either side of the entrance.

Boone looked at the guard that remained, tempted to have Vanessa stick a knife into his thigh from a hundred feet away. Instead, he asked if the guard had observed any unusual activity.

The guard shook his head. "The boy came back to the coach awhile ago and nobody has left the coach."

"What about the woman across the street?"

"The paparazzi dame? She's still there as far as I know."

Boone shook his head. "Car's there, but she's not."

The guard shrugged. "Probably went to get something to eat. I don't expect we'll have much activity until the talent gets back here this afternoon. We'll be ready for them."

Boone turned away and walked into the coach before he said something he might regret. Vanessa followed him inside. He wasn't at all surprised to see that the coach was empty. He lifted the sofa cushion and stared at the open hatch beneath it. Vanessa walked into the master suite to search it while Boone tore out the three bugs and dropped them into a cold mug of coffee left over from breakfast.

"We're clear," he said. "We can talk."

Vanessa came out of the master suite with Q's BlackBerry. "Three missed calls," she said. "All from Blaze."

"This is an all-time record for us," Boone said. "We've managed to lose four injured Mossad agents and two kids in less than two hours. I should have pulled the plug on this thing last night."

Vanessa shook her head. "We already covered that territory. You made the right decision. We'll find them."

Boone still wasn't sure about the decision, but Vanessa was right...they had to find Q and Angela...and soon. Roger and Blaze would be flying back to Philadelphia in a few hours and he didn't want to tell them that he had lost their children.

"Call the guys off bus duty and bring them up to speed. Tell them to bring Croc to the building next door and start again from there. But before they come have him drop Uly at Carma's hotel. I want him and Everett to go in hard. If Devorah shows tell them to hold them there until I call."

"Everett and Uly will enjoy that," Vanessa said.

Boone's BlackBerry rang. He looked at the screen. He didn't want to answer it, but he knew he didn't have a choice.

"Hi, Heather," he said.

"I know I'm never supposed to ask, but what is going on there,

Boone?"

Heather Hughes was one of Boone's oldest friends, and his staunchest supporter. She was one of the few people who knew about his former double life as a NOC agent for the CIA. She had learned of it by mistake thirty years earlier and had kept it a secret all that time. He had called her about becoming Blaze and Roger's personal driver. Heather was the one who had told Buddy T. to hire him for the job. It was no coincidence that Match's first concert was at the Electric Factory in the same city where Malak Tucker had allegedly perished. Boone had asked Heather to arrange it. And she had with no questions asked.

"You don't want to know, Heather," Boone answered.

"No I don't…but I've got two very worried parents here whose children haven't answered their calls and they want to know why. What can I tell them?"

"Where are you?" Boone asked.

"Chicago. Roger and Blaze are in their dressing room getting ready for Oprah. I flew in from LA this morning…and Buddy—the little toad—says he'll try to squeeze me onto the jet this afternoon so I can be at the Electric Factory for the concert tonight."

"I guess I need a bigger jet," Boone said.

Heather laughed. "I figured the jet was yours. That's going to save Match a lot of money."

"We're charging them for it to make it look good," Boone said. "But I'll figure out a way to get the fee back into their account."

"Initially you said that all you wanted to do was ride with them to Philly. I assume that things have changed."

"Dramatically," Boone said.

"Do you know what you're doing, Boone?"

"Yes, I know what I'm doing," Boone answered. "I just don't know what everybody else is doing. But I'll figure it out."

"When you retired," Heather said. "My life got a lot simpler."

"Mine too," Boone said. "But what I'm doing now is a lot more important than what I did back then. And trust me, the less you know about it the better off you'll be."

"I trust you, Boone, but I still need something to tell the frantic parents."

"Tell them that the cell phones I got them malfunctioned and I had to take them back to the store to get fixed. We've been taking in the sights, going to museums, movies where they don't allow cell phones, which is why I missed their calls. You were lucky to catch me at the concession stand getting some popcorn for the kids."

"In other words," Heather said, "lie."

"Exactly." Boone noticed the laptop lying on the master suite bed. He opened it and saw that he needed a password to boot it up. "Hang on a sec, Heather." He muted the call.

"Get X in here," he told Vanessa.

"He's not going to be happy about that," Vanessa said. "You know what he's like when his equipment is down."

"I don't care!" Boone snapped. "I want him in here right now!"

Boone got back on with Heather. "I need a couple of things," he said.

"Name them."

"Hardened security," Boone said. "These guys Buddy T. hired are worthless. We need professionals. People we can trust. Tell Buddy T. you want me to be in charge of tour security. I'll get the right people."

"Buddy T.'s not going to buy that. What does an old roadie like *you know about tour security?"*

"Tell him while he was in New York these morons let someone into the motor coach, which is the truth. If Roger or Blaze found out they'd go ballistic. I'll keep it between the three of us if he turns security over to me."

"He'll probably go along with that. What's the second thing?"

"Your flight is going to be late leaving Chicago. Mechanical problems. I want Roger and Blaze back here at the last possible moment. Ideally, I don't even want them to have the time to stop at the motor coach. I want the limo to take them directly to the Electric Factory from the airport."

"You're starting to make me really nervous, Boone."

Boone had no soothing words for her. "Is Marie or Art around?"

"I just saw Marie. Let me find her. By the way, Roger and Blaze are absolutely wild about them. I assumed they worked for you. Who would have thought a couple of spooks could be such great personal assistants. I just might start recruiting PAs from the CIA."

"The way things are going in the CIA these days," Boone said. "You'd probably get a lot of takers."

"Here she is… Marie, it's for you."

Boone told Marie to call the pilots and arrange the bogus mechanical problem. She asked him what was going on just as X came into the coach with a sour look on his face.

"I'll tell you later." Boone ended the call.

"I'm kind of busy," X complained. "What do you need?"

Boone handed him the laptop. "A password."

"Whose laptop?"

"I don't know, but I think it's Angela's."

X started typing in possible passwords one after another.

"*Don't you have a program that can do that?*" *Vanessa asked.*

"*Yeah,*" *X said.* "*And it could take two hours to crack the password using it. I assume you're in a hurry.*" *As his fingers flew over the keys he told them about the virus.* "*I think it might have been better if they had used a bullet. I've never seen anything like it. It might take a week to untangle it…if I can untangle it. And I think while they were at it they uploaded all of our data.*"

"*Everything?*"

"*I won't know until everything's back online,*" *X said, still typing.* "*But yeah, I think they now have everything we had. Ah…that was it.*"

Angela's screen came to life. She hadn't closed the exchange she'd had with Q. Boone, Vanessa, and X crowded around the screen and read every word.

"*Get Felix in here,*" *Boone said.* "*We're going to have to proceed carefully or Malak will bolt. And we're not going to have the advantage of X's surveillance equipment.*"

"*It'll be just like the old days,*" *Vanessa said with a little smile.* "*And if you remember, we were pretty good at it.*"

"*Once upon a time,*" *Boone said grimly.*

While Vanessa called the others Boone asked X what the password was.

"*November 30, 2004,*" *X answered.* "*No spaces.*"

Liberty Bell

"See?" I said. "That wasn't so bad."

It had taken us a grand total of seven minutes to reach Independence Hall, and as far as I could tell, we hadn't been followed. But it was obvious by the way Angela was scanning our surroundings she was not nearly as certain as I was. We were sitting on a bench outside the hall and there were a lot of people around. School groups, tourists, street people—there were even a couple of policemen on foot patrol.

"It's almost three," Angela said, looking at her watch. "Maybe we missed her."

I shook my head. "We're not that late. She didn't tell us exactly where to meet her outside Independence Hall and this is a big place. Your mom wouldn't have gone to this much trouble and not show because we were a few minutes late."

Angela sighed. "What if it isn't my mom?"

It seemed to me that I had brought this possibility up more than once. "If it isn't your mom then we're in huge trouble and I hope they taught you in your martial arts class how to defend yourself–and more importantly me–against a terrorist leopard."

Angela smiled and was about to say something when a policeman limped up and sat down on the other side of her. This was about the last person in the world we wanted to join us on the bench, but we couldn't very well get up and rush away without looking guilty of something. It was a school day. I figured he was going to ask us what we were doing there alone. But if that was going to be his question he decided to ease into it.

"A beautiful day to visit Independence Hall," he said.

It was actually overcast and looked like it might rain. He looked like he was in his mid-fifties, a little overweight, with blue eyes, and spoke with a slight accent.

"Have you been into Independence Hall before?" he asked.

"Yes," Angela answered.

He looked at the old brick building for a second then said, "A great deal of history was made beyond those walls. Decisions that changed the world. Courageous sacrifices that are still changing the world."

"Like the Declaration of Independence," I said.

The policeman nodded. "Did you know that the men who signed that document were considered traitors by the British? Now they're heroes and the Brits are your staunchest allies. The passage of time changes everything. You fought the Germans and the Japanese in World War II, now they're your allies too. I guess it's just the natural ebb and flow of history. Evil people wash ashore with evil ideologies. We clean them up…and wait to see what the next tide brings."

I'd never had a conversation with a Philadelphia cop (or any cop for that matter) but this seemed like a weird thing to say to a couple of kids sitting on a bench.

"It would be nice if we could just skip the war part," he continued. "But the maniacs and fanatics and their blind followers usually make this impossible." He nodded at the old brick building. "Even in more recent times sacrifices have been made inside that Hall. Decisions that were so audacious and bold that even the passage of time might not uncover the truth of what happened."

I was getting nervous…or I should say, more nervous… and it wasn't because he was a cop. It was because I was beginning to think he *wasn't* a cop. "…*your* staunchest allies…. *You* fought the Germans and the Japanese…." He should have said *our* and *we.* Where was *he* from?

I looked at my watch. "Wow," I said. "We're late! We were supposed to meet Mom and Dad fifteen minutes ago."

I stood up, fully expecting Angela to join me, but she remained planted on the bench, staring at the policeman through her dark sunglasses. Apparently her highly tuned Secret Service-trained brain had gone deaf. She hadn't heard the Liberty Bell alarm clanging that this guy is not a cop, so therefore he's a terrorist or Mossad agent. "The redcoats are coming! The redcoats are coming!" I wanted to shout. But in this case the red uniform was blue.

"We have to go," I insisted. "You know how worried Mom gets when we're late." I would have yanked Angela off the bench, but I was afraid she might plant her foot in my ear.

The policeman looked at me. "Your mother is in Chicago," he said. He looked at Angela. "And *your* mother is down the street. Waiting."

"Who are you?" Angela asked quietly.

"You can call me Ziv," he answered.

Angela stood up (finally). "You're with Eben Lavi! You're with the Mossad!"

"I was with Eben Lavi," he said calmly. "But I was never with the Mossad, although they believe that I was."

"Where's Eben?" Angela asked.

"He's gone dark," Ziv answered. "He's off the grid. Do you know what that means?"

Angela and I shook our heads.

"He has resigned from the Mossad and is working on his own. He's a rogue agent...for the time being. Or maybe permanently. Who knows?"

"Is he still in Philadelphia?" Angela asked.

"I suspect he is."

"What does he want?" Angela asked.

"He wants to kill a leopard. He wants to avenge his brother."

"Aaron," Angela said.

Ziv nodded. "But he's after the wrong person. The leopard did not murder Aaron. Salim Kazi and Amun Massri took Aaron's life."

So the second guy at the Paris café and the boy who tried to blow up Independence Hall was named Amun Massri. Boone and his team would be interested in that information.

"Salim Kazi was killed in Tijuana three weeks ago," I said.

"Eben killed him."

Angela turned to me, and even though I couldn't see her eyes under the shades I could tell she was glaring.

"Mr. Boone is well-informed," Ziv said. "But that is not correct. Eben had nothing to do with Salim Kazi's death." He smiled. "That pleasure was all mine."

A chill ran down my spine. Boone had said that Salim Kazi had been beaten and tortured before he died.

"Who do you work for?" Angela asked.

"I work for the good of mankind," Ziv answered.

Salim Kazi probably didn't agree with that, I thought.

"I'm serious," Angela said sharply.

"I am being serious," Ziv said. "I'm the monkey that watches the leopard's tail. I'm her second pair of eyes and ears. I make certain that no one stalks her while she stalks her prey. But she's a good leopard. She only kills those who deserve to die. Aaron Lavi was not one of them, but she could not stop Salim and Amun without compromising herself."

"You tapped into the bugs that Eben planted in our bus," I said.

Ziv shook his head. "We could have, but there was no need to since I was working with Eben, Devorah, and Carma at the time—or so they thought."

"Where are Devorah and Carma?" I asked.

"I ordered them to return home, but like Eben, I doubt they obeyed. They're trying to make a name for themselves. And they can't do that by returning to the Institute with a failed mission and their tails between their legs. Carma and Devorah will try to get together, if they aren't already together, and see what they can salvage from the mess we've created for them. I think Eben will remain on his own. He's had enough of those two."

"You said my mother was waiting for me," Angela said. "That means she's alive."

"Indeed she is, but I've already said too much."

"Does Eben know that my mother had an identical twin?" Angela asked.

"No he doesn't," Ziv answered. "That's a very carefully guarded secret and the reason we're all here." He looked at his watch. "You must go. But I have a request before I tell you where she's waiting."

"What is it?" Angela asked.

"I assume your cell phones have tracking abilities."

Angela nodded.

"And I assume you disabled your cell phones so Mr. Boone could not follow you here."

Again Angela nodded.

"Did either of you bring your cell phone with you?"

"I left mine back in the bus," I said, wishing now I had palmed it, which I could have easily done without Angela noticing.

"I have mine," Angela said.

"I need to borrow it."

"Why?"

"To make sure you don't turn it on when you meet your mother," Ziv answered. "And to lead the SOS team in the opposite direction. She doesn't want to meet Mr. Boone at this time."

"And if I say no?" Angela asked.

"Then I'm afraid we will have to part ways," Ziv answered. "Your mother has risked everything by contacting you–against my advice, by the way. Now it's your turn to take a risk."

Angela handed over her BlackBerry and its battery.

Ziv told us where the leopard was waiting.

Ziv watched the children walk away. He waited a few minutes, then got up from the bench, leaving Angela's BlackBerry and battery behind concealed beneath a newspaper. A few minutes later another man walked up to the bench and slipped the BlackBerry and battery into his pocket. The man was the leopard's second monkey.

Rogue

"You know," I said after we'd walked half a block in complete silence, "it might not have been such a good idea to give him our only mode of communication."

"I know," Angela said. "But he wouldn't have told us where to go if I hadn't. And he took your word that you left your BlackBerry back at the coach. You did leave it back there?"

"Unfortunately," I said, still kicking myself.

"I think he would have searched you if he thought you were lying. That means he trusted you. I think we can trust him."

I laughed.

"What's so funny?"

"Boone gave me the same lecture this morning," I answered, without elaborating.

"I feel bad about setting up Boone," Angela said. "As soon as he picks up my cell signal he's going to come running and he's not going to be happy when he finds the phone without us."

"After your ditching Felix at the hotel and my leaving the coach without telling Boone I doubt he's capable of getting madder than he already is. If we were six-year-olds he'd probably spank us."

"I wouldn't blame him," Angela said.

We were headed to familiar territory—the restaurant across the street from the dry cleaner where we had first spotted Eben. There were apartments above the restaurant. Ziv said that Angela's mother would be waiting behind door #3.

Angela was still keeping an eye out for a tail, but not nearly as carefully as she had before. She was either eager to get this over with (like I was) or she was confident that Ziv had somehow cleared the way for us.

"So you trust Ziv," I said.

"I don't think he's working with Eben, if that's what you mean," she said. "He would have grabbed us at Independence Hall. No one would bat an eye at a policeman hauling off two kids. So I guess I do trust him." She paused. "It's weird. As soon as he started talking I felt a connection with him. It was almost like I knew him, a familiarity that I can't explain."

"That is weird," I said. "Especially after he told us what a pleasure it was to murder Salim Kazi in Mexico. I don't know about you, but I've never met a murderer, at least anyone who bragged about it."

"I don't think he was bragging," Angela said.

"Confessing murder to two total strangers is bragging," I said. "Do you think Ziv and your mother are working alone?"

"I don't know," Angela said. "I just hope that it's my mom.

And you don't have to come with me, Q. This is not your problem. It would be safer if you went back to the…"

Eben stepped out in front of us with a knife. He grabbed me by the arm before I could react and held the sharp blade against my ribcage. Angela's fast feet and hands weren't going to work this time. It didn't look like either of us were going to make it to door #3.

The Ten of Hearts

I'd be lying if I said I wasn't absolutely terrified. And it wasn't just the knife tip stuck between my second and third ribs. It was the way Eben looked. The night before when he followed Angela he looked feral and predatory. Now he looked feral, predatory, and very, very angry. His appearance wasn't helped by the hideous black eye and his bruised, swollen jaw. If anyone needed sunglasses to disguise himself, it was Eben Lavi.

"Let him go!" Angela shouted.

"If you raise your voice again," Eben hissed, "or attempt to run away I will kill him."

He pulled me through a doorway. Angela followed. Eben kicked the door closed behind us. We were in an abandoned restaurant with booths and tables layered with dust and rat droppings. Eben must have been following us from the beginning. He had gotten ahead of us, broken into the restaurant, then waited.

"This has nothing to do with Q," Angela said.

"It did not seem that way last night." He pulled the ten of hearts out of his pocket and flipped it onto a table. "Sit."

Angela sat on the edge of a filthy bench.

Eben didn't offer me a seat nor did he take the knife away. He was obviously leery of Angela after what she had done to him the night before, which was no doubt why he had grabbed me instead of her. I needed to learn taekwondo.

"Dump the contents of your backpack on the table," he demanded.

Angela did as she was told. This is not the way I wanted to learn what she carried around in the tattered old pack. Among the pile were several pairs of sunglasses, a thick pocketbook, a notebook, an iPod, a set of earphones, pencils and pens, two paperbacks, and the photo of her mother. Nothing of any consequence, making me wonder why she bothered to carry the pack at all. But Eben was interested in the photo. He picked it up and looked at it for a moment, then slipped it into his pocket.

"Give the photo back!" Angela said.

"Empty your pockets," Eben said.

She turned her pockets inside out. The only thing inside was one yellow origami crane made from a McDonald's cheeseburger wrapper.

"Satisfied?" Angela said. "Now give me the photo back."

I wished she would stop using that sharp tone of voice. I was the one with the sharp knife digging into my side.

"I'm going to keep the photo," Eben said. "And I am far from satisfied." He stepped behind me, grabbed the collar of my shirt, and put the point of the knife on the side of my neck.

He glared at Angela. "Stand up and turn around."

"Why?" Angela asked.

Instead of answering, Eben dug the tip into my neck.

"Ouch!" I tried to pull away.

He held me fast and said, "I wouldn't make any sudden moves. This knife is very sharp."

I froze.

Angela turned her back to us, but not before I felt a trickle of blood roll down my neck. Eben reached into his pocket with his free hand and pulled out a coil of rope.

"Tie her wrists," he said. "Tightly. I'm watching."

Angela turned her head and looked at me. I winked and gave her a nervous grin, hoping she got the message. I knew dozens of interesting knots. I tied her wrists.

Eben inspected my handiwork. Angela really had him spooked. He was treating her like he thought *she* was the leopard, not her mother.

"Sit back down," he said, then (to my relief) he shoved me onto the bench across from her. He wiped my blood off the tip of the knife onto his pants.

"I am going to ask you some questions and if you don't answer them to my satisfaction I will kill the boy."

"Have you ever killed a boy?" Angela asked.

"Yes," Eben said. "Young girls too. And you'll be next if I don't get the answers I want."

I was about ready to murder Angela myself. She needed to drop the 'tude. Had she forgotten that Eben was an assassin?

Eben yanked her sunglasses off and tossed them on the

dusty table.

"What did the policeman at Independence Hall say to you?" he asked.

I was right. Eben had been following us and had set a trap. I hoped Carma and Devorah weren't nearby.

"Ziv said that you were off the grid," Angela answered calmly.

"He told you his name was Ziv?" Eben seemed surprised.

Angela nodded. "He said that you were a rogue agent and that we should go back to the warehouse where we would be safe."

"Did he tell you who he was working for?"

Angela looked confused, and I have to say the look was pretty convincing. "He's working for the Mossad just like you *were*. He told us that you went off the deep end."

"Why was he wearing a police uniform?"

"He knew he wouldn't be able to approach us otherwise," Angela answered without the slightest hesitation. She must have a black belt in lying as well as taekwondo. She was better at it than Boone was.

"Why did he take your phone?"

Uh-oh...

"He wanted to make contact with Tyrone Boone and tell him–"

The knife came down with a *bang* stabbing the ten of hearts dead center. "I warned you about lying." He pulled the knife out of the card. "If you lie again I will put this knife in your brother's heart."

Angela went pale and bit her lower lip.

"Why did he take your phone?" Eben repeated, taking a step closer to me.

Now would be a good time to tell the truth, I thought, or surprise him by jumping up and breaking his neck with her hands that weren't really tied.

"He wanted to lead Boone away from us," Angela answered.

"Why?"

I thought Angela might bite off her lower lip. Eben was in easy range of Angela's lightning foot. I willed her to remember my wink and smile, but she just sat there. She hadn't gotten the message.

"Angela's mom didn't kill your brother," I blurted out. "He was killed by two terrorists named Salim Kazi and Amun Massri. Ziv killed Salim Kazi a few weeks ago in Mexico."

Eben stared at me for a second, then closed his good eye and nodded as if this somehow made sense.

"Ziv told me he had been pulled off an assignment in Mexico to join us," he said almost to himself, then looked back at me. "Did he say where Amun was?"

I shook my head.

"I'm going to ask you again," Eben said slowly. "Who is he working for?"

"The good of mankind," Angela answered.

He took a step toward me. "I warned you."

"It's the truth!" I said. "That's what he told us." I didn't mention the monkey and leopard tail thing.

"Is the leopard in Philadelphia?" Eben asked.

"Huh?" I said.

"What are you talking about?" Angela said.

"Your mother," Eben said impatiently. "Malak. Also known as Anmar, or the leopard."

"My mother is dead!" Angela said indignantly. "She was killed four years ago in the line of duty. She was a Secret Service agent."

"*Was* is the key word," Eben said. "Now she's a terrorist."

"My mother died on November 30, 2004 right here in Philadelphia at Independence Hall. She is not a terrorist. She was killed by a terrorist bomb."

Eben shook his head. "I don't believe you."

"I do," Boone said.

This time I was happy to be startled. Boone had slipped in like a ghost through the swinging door in the back of the restaurant. The automatic pistol he held looked out of place, but the old hand holding it was as steady as a rock. Croc stood next to Boone drilling his weird blue eye into Eben's head.

Eben was about three feet away from me and appeared to be considering his options. The front door opened and in stepped Felix, also holding an automatic pistol, eliminating all of Eben's options. Apparently Ziv's BlackBerry ruse hadn't worked. Boone must have followed us from Independence Hall, or else he had tapped into Eben's cell phone signal totally ignoring Angela's BlackBerry signal.

"Drop the knife," Felix said.

Eben hesitated, then dropped the knife.

"Give the photo back to Angela," Boone said.

Slowly, Eben pulled the photo out of his pocket and tossed it onto the dusty table.

Angela stood up. "Untie me," she said.

"Just pull your wrists apart," I told her.

She did and the cord fell to the ground.

"Why didn't you say something?"

"I tried to," I said, giving her an exaggerated wink, which she totally ignored...again.

Boone noticed the blood on my neck and the collar of my shirt. A look came over his face I hadn't seen before...rage. He raised his pistol and pointed it at Eben's head.

"I guess you win this round," Eben said, relatively calmly under the circumstances.

"We have won all the rounds," Boone said. "And now the fight is over. You lost."

For a second I thought Boone was going to pull the trigger. Instead, he let out a long breath and looked at us. "Vanessa is waiting for you in the van in back of the restaurant. You can cut through the kitchen. She'll drive you to the warehouse."

"What are you going to do?" Angela asked.

"We're going to have a private conversation with our Mossad friend here and we'll join you later."

Angela and I hesitated.

"Go!" Boone said. "Now!"

Angela pushed her stuff into her backpack and slung it over her shoulder.

I followed her into a gutted kitchen with Croc at my heels.

"I can't believe I wasn't really tied," Angela said as we walked through the kitchen to the back door. "If I'd known that I could have done something about Eben before Boone showed up."

"I winked at you when I tied your hands," I protested. "I don't know how you could have missed it."

Angela stopped and looked at me. "You are wearing dark sunglasses, Q."

"Oh." I guess I was so scared I forgot I had them on.

"What do you think they're going to do to Eben?" Angela asked.

"I don't know." I touched the side of my neck where he had stuck me. "And I'm not sure I care."

She looked at the cut. "It's not deep. He knew exactly where to stick you without severing an artery. I think he was just trying to scare me."

"Scare you?" I said.

Angela was biting her lower lip again.

"Okay," I said. "What's on your mind?"

"I'm not going back to the warehouse," she said.

"I figured that."

"I have to follow this through. It's my only chance."

I nodded and peeked out the back window. "Here's something interesting," I said.

She joined me at the window.

The van was nowhere to be seen.

"Nice weapon," Eben said, nodding at Boone's automatic.

"Found it in a car in the desert," Boone said. "Sit down and keep your hands on the table where we can see them."

Eben took a seat. "You have no legal authority to hold me. I have diplomatic immunity."

"We're not exactly sticklers for legality," Felix said. "And nobody is immune. We operate off the books and have our own rules."

"And you broke one of those rules when you drew blood on a thirteen-year-old boy," Boone added tightly.

"For what it's worth," Eben said. "It was just a small nick. I wouldn't have taken it any further. I don't kill children. I was trying to get them to talk. If I were you I'd be more concerned about my two female team members."

"We were concerned about them," Boone said. "That's why two of our men have them under guard right now in Carma's hotel room. Your partners are not happy. What we do with them depends on what happens here in the next few minutes. Their fate is in your hands."

Eben didn't particularly care about Carma and Devorah's fate, but as fellow Mossad agents—as horrible as they were—he was obligated to help them if he could.

"Who are you?" Eben asked.

Boone told him.

When he finished, Eben gave him a small smile and said, "I doubt you'll answer this, but were you able to find out anything about my former driver?"

"Ziv?" Boone said. "Not a lot, but we were able to pick up some of his conversation in Independence Park with Angela and Q, using parabolic microphones."

"Ancient technology," Eben said.

"Our new technology was sabotaged, but the old stuff worked fine. For instance we learned that Ziv infiltrated your team and that he works for Malak Tucker."

"You mean the leopard," Eben said. "Do you know where Ziv is?"

"Yes," Boone said. "We have him under surveillance." He stared at Eben for a few moments, deciding how much more to tell him. "What is your status with the Mossad?"

Eben laughed. "I thought I officially resigned this afternoon, but it appears that I gave the resignation letter I've been carrying around for months to my enemy. That blunder by itself is enough for the Mossad to terminate me even if I didn't want to resign. So, one way or the other, I am no longer working for the Mossad. They just don't know it yet."

Felix stepped forward and tossed Eben's resignation letter on the table next to the ten of hearts. "One of our guys found it in Ziv's hospital room."

"What are you going to do?" Boone asked.

Eben picked up the envelope. "I guess my fate is in your hands too," he said. "I want to eliminate the people responsible for my brother's *death, then I want to send this in."*

"I have a different scenario in mind," Boone said. "One of the men responsible for Aaron's death has already been eliminated. Malak Tucker, or Anmar, did not kill your brother."

"So I've been told," Eben said. "But I'm not convinced."

"If I can convince you," Boone said. "Would you be willing to get Carma and Devorah to back off?"

Eben thought about it for a moment, then said, "I'd try."

Boone tucked the automatic into the waistband of his jeans. Felix kept his gun in his beefy hand.

"I want you to listen to something," Boone said. "First I'm going to play an interview I conducted with Angela. When it's over I'll play the conversation we picked up at Independence Hall between the kids and your old teammate, Ziv.

Boone pulled his digital tape recorder out of his backpack and set it on the table, then pushed the play button...

"If you don't mind I'm going to refer to your mother by her given name."

"All right," Angela said.

"What did the Secret Service tell you about Malak's death..."

Door #3

"Why do you think Boone lied about the van?" Angela asked.

We were walking down the street toward the restaurant with Croc in between us.

I shook my head. "I don't know," I said.

"Do you think SOS is following us?" she asked.

"Absolutely," I said. "Boone must have followed us from Independence Hall. He wasn't fooled by Ziv's BlackBerry trick."

"I never saw them," Angela said. "And we know what they look like. It's incredible."

"Yeah, I think Boone and his old spy buddies are better at this than we thought."

"So, we're leading them right to my mom," Angela said.

"That would be my guess. I just hope we aren't leading Carma and Devorah to her. We can always head back to the warehouse."

"I can't," Angela said. "Not now. But if we catch anyone following us we'll go back to the coach."

I looked at my watch. It was already after five. Roger and Mom were probably back at the coach wondering where we were. There was a good chance that Malak would no longer be waiting for us behind door #3. We were late and that could only mean that we'd had trouble. She wasn't going to stick around and wait for us to bring the trouble to her.

We stopped outside the restaurant. To the right of the entrance was a door that looked like it led to apartments above.

"Wait here," Angela said.

"Where are you going?"

"I'm going to check out the people in the restaurant and make sure there isn't anyone I recognize. I'll be right back."

Croc sat down next to me. I looked up and down the street and didn't see anything unusual, but there were dozens of apartments above old storefronts. A hundred pairs of eyes could be watching us beyond the dark windows, I thought.

Angela came back out. "I think we're clear. There were only a few people eating and I didn't see anyone I recognized."

"Probably getting a bite to eat before the Match concert," I said. "Which starts in about an hour and forty-five minutes."

"Let's go up," Angela said nervously.

We walked up a narrow flight of creaky stairs. At the top was a long hallway with rows of doors on either side. The smells of the restaurant kitchen filled the hallway, but it didn't make me hungry. Food was the last thing I was concerned about.

Angela and I walked slowly down the hallway with Croc

following.

13... 12... 11...

"It's not too late to change your mind," I whispered.

10... 9... 8... 7...

"We've come this far," she whispered back.

6... 5... 4...

We stopped in front of door #3.

It was ajar.

I looked at Angela. She was biting her lower lip. She nodded. I pushed the door open. The old apartment was completely empty except for a single chair facing the door. Sitting in the chair was...

"What are you doing here!" Angela shouted.

I was too shocked to speak.

"What took you so long?" Dirk Peski asked.

He was holding Angela's phone in one hand and the battery to it in the other.

Croc growled.

Dirk

"Were you followed?" Dirk asked.

"I don't understand," Angela said.

"It's a pretty simple question," Dirk said.

"What Angela means," I said, "is that we don't understand what you have to do with all this."

"That should be obvious," Dirk said. "I work with Malak–better known in anti-terrorists circles as the leopard–and Ziv…although that's not his real name, which you've probably already figured out."

"Where's my mother?" Angela asked.

"She's waiting for you. But before I tell you where, you need to tell me what took you so long to get here."

I told him.

When I finished Dirk looked at Croc and grinned. Croc did not grin back. "I told them that Boone was a pro," he said. "So, when you got to the back of the restaurant the van wasn't there."

"Right," I said.

"Then you were followed," Dirk said. "But Ziv didn't pick them up and he's pretty good. Boone has almost passed the last test."

"What test?" Angela asked.

"You'll see," Dirk said. He stood up and handed her the phone. "I'd better hang onto the battery for awhile. Don't want to make it too easy for Boone."

"We don't know where Carma and Devorah are," I said, thinking he should know just in case they were lurking around.

"I know where they are and so does Boone," Dirk said. "Everett and Uly are holding them hostage in Carma's room. They caught up with Devorah on her way to the hotel. That only leaves Vanessa and Ray unaccounted for. But I suspect they're nearby. Which reminds me..." He reached into his pocket and pulled out a flash drive. "When you see Ray tell him all he has to do is stick this thing into the computer's USB port and everything will come back online." He gave me the flash drive.

"You took out the intellimobile?" I said.

Dirk laughed. "Is that what they call it?"

"Yeah."

"You're right," he said. "We took it out, but just temporarily. We wanted to know how SOS would do with the electronic rug pulled out from under them. You can also tell Ray that most of the information that we swiped we already knew. The flash drive will restore the data plus a couple of bits of information he might find interesting."

Dirk looked at his watch. "There isn't much time. Go down

to room thirteen. And don't let the number spook you. The leopard has more luck than she knows what do with. Nine lives and all that."

As Dirk walked past us he stopped and patted the still growling Croc on his broad head, then gave us another grin. "Yep, old Boone's pretty good. See you kids down the road."

We watched him walk down the hallway. He paused outside the last room, slipped something under the door, then we heard him trot down the stairs.

"Thirteen," Angela said.

Door #13

The woman with the spiky blond hair was standing in the empty apartment. She was on her cell phone when we walked in. She snapped it closed. Angela and she stared at each other frozen for several seconds. The gold angel leopard necklace hung around the woman's neck. Her hand began tapping her right thigh. Then the tears came.

They met in the middle of the room and threw their arms around each other. There was no doubt in my mind that this was Malak, the angel, Angela's mother. I picked up the BlackBerry battery Dirk had slipped under the door and waited.

Malak finally let her daughter go and walked over to me. "I'm Malak Tucker." She gave me a hug too, but not nearly as intense as the one she gave Angela. "It's good to meet you, Q."

She certainly didn't act like a terrorist, or a Secret Service agent (although I hadn't met anyone with either of those occupations). There was a genuine warmth to her that wasn't reflected in the photo Angela carried in her backpack.

She looked at her watch. "I'm afraid we have very little time, Angela. If I don't leave here soon things could go very bad for me."

"I'll wait out in the hallway and let you talk," I said, starting toward the door.

"No," Malak said. "This concerns you too." She looked at Angela. "First, I am so sorry for what I did to you and your dad. But I'll be honest… If I had to do it all over again I would make the same decision. I had no choice. I hope you'll understand someday and forgive me."

Angela was too choked up to respond.

"Before I leave I need some questions answered." Malak looked at me. "Who does Boone and his SOS team work for?"

I told her what Boone had told me.

"And this man he said he was working for," she said. "Did Boone mention his name?"

"He said his name is Mr. Potus," I answered. "But I'm sure that wasn't his real name."

"Of course!" Malak said, smiling. "And that's where I remember Boone from. I remembered his face, but I couldn't place him. Do you know who Mr. Potus is?"

I shook my head.

"Potus stands for 'president of the United States'."

"You mean J.R. Culpepper?" I thought back to Boone passing his cell phone to Mr. Little at Independence Hall. No wonder Mr. Little changed his attitude so quickly.

"When I was on presidential duty," Malak continued,

"J.R. was the vice president. Boone came to the White House for an intelligence briefing. Because of the way he looked I was pretty hard on him before we let him into the oval office to meet with the president and J.R."

"He mentioned that," I said.

Malak smiled again. "I bet he did."

"Before J.R. became a senator, then VP and president," she explained, "he was the director of the CIA. I got the impression that he and Boone were pretty tight. I spent a lot of time with J.R. before he became president. I liked him. He had very few illusions about how our government actually works. It's all making sense now. Did Boone mention if anyone else knows about me?"

Angela found her voice. "I got the impression this was just between them," she said. "And that they were going to keep it that way until they figured out what was going on."

"Good," Malak said. "But even if they *think* they know what's going on they need to keep it between themselves. Tell Boone that this goes deeper than he and President Culpepper can imagine. Virtually every intelligence agency in every country has been compromised. There are terrorists working in every one of them and some of them are in very high positions."

"How did that happen?" I asked.

"Billions of dollars and thirty years of intrigue is how it happened," Malak answered. "My twin sister, Anmar, was part of it…and I was supposed to be too."

"What do you mean?" Angela asked.

"A few years before the explosion at Independence Hall, Anmar was sent to a rally for the president when I was agent in charge. You can imagine her shock when she saw a Secret Service agent who was a mirror image of herself. She didn't tell her then-husband…her handler, or anyone else. Two years before the explosion at Independence Hall she contacted me and told me that she had been adopted and brought to the U.S. just like I had.

"Our real mother died during childbirth. Our real father was told that we died as well. We were put with families that immigrated to the U.S. legally. When I turned eighteen my adoptive parents arranged a marriage for me. I would have none of it and left home. Anmar made a different decision. She married the man her adoptive parents had picked for her and this is when her terrorist training began."

"So, she was a terrorist," I said.

"A very good one," Malak said. "But she had a change of heart and wanted out. That's why she approached me. She couldn't leave on her own. Once a terrorist always a terrorist. They don't let you go. She needed protection, a new identity…" Malak paused. "I talked her out of leaving." She looked at Angela. "That is my second biggest regret."

Malak went on to tell us that it was Anmar who had given her the information about the bombings in the U.S. and abroad. She couldn't give up her source without endangering her twin sister. When she rushed to Independence Hall on November 30, 2004 Malak was about to be fired and Anmar was on the verge of being exposed and murdered.

"I drove to Philadelphia to stop the bombing and take my sister into protective custody," Malak said. "But I arrived too late." Tears welled in her eyes. "When I walked into the hall she was trying to defuse the bomb. If I had brought her in sooner she would be alive today. I decided the only way to honor Anmar was to take her place. I knew everything about her. All the people she knew, who her handlers were and how they contacted her—"

"What about her husband?" Angela asked.

Malak hesitated before answering. "He was killed before I met him. I got to play the grieving widow, which was a great cover for why I wasn't quite myself that first year I became Anmar."

I looked at Angela. She was biting her lower lip, but I knew she wasn't going to ask: Who killed Anmar's husband? And neither was I. Some questions are best left unasked. I was certain that Malak had done some terrible things in the past several years to convince her fellow terrorists that she was who she said she was and to maintain her cover.

The door opened and Boone stepped inside.

Malak did not act at all surprised to see him. "Mr. Boone," she said, but the warmth from the moment before was completely gone. She had instantly turned into the photo of the woman at the firing range.

"It's a pleasure to see you again," Boone said.

Malak looked at him for a moment then said, "You passed the test."

"What test?" Boone asked.

"We'll call it a security test," Malak answered. "I had to be sure you were good before I brought you into this."

"And what have you brought me into?"

"Armageddon, unless we're able to stop it."

Armageddon

"They're about to unleash everything they've been setting up here in the U.S. for the past thirty years," Malak explained. "It's scheduled to start in the Capital the day after tomorrow."

"The ghost cell," Boone said.

Malak nodded. "And these are really scary ghosts." She looked at her watch. "In three minutes I'm leaving here. Where's Eben?"

"He's on his way over to the hotel to strike a deal with Carma and Devorah. Your identity is safe. And I've convinced him to come work for me."

"You trust him?"

"I do."

"Tell him that under no circumstances is he to harm, or even approach Amun Massri if he runs across him. The same goes for you and all of your people. Amun is the key to this whole thing. For the moment he's an untouchable."

"Got it," Boone said. "But Amun isn't very good at this. There are three photos of him now. One when he was young at Independence Hall, one at the Paris café, and one at Fisherman's Wharf."

"He's young, careless, and very dangerous, but I think he has the ear of the head of this cell." She held up her hand. "Before you ask, I don't know who that is…yet. But I'm getting close to finding out."

Malak looked at her watch again. "Here are the rules and they are non-negotiable. Any information I have I will pass through either Angela or Q. You and I, Boone, will rarely meet."

"Why bring the kids into this?" Boone asked.

"Because that's the only way you'll stay on to protect them, Roger, and Blaze." She turned to Angela. "And just so you know… I couldn't be happier for your dad. He's found a wonderful woman in Blaze and she's found a wonderful man. Malak Tucker is dead and we are going to have to leave it that way for your sake and theirs. I know it's a huge burden for you to carry, but there's no choice."

She turned back to Boone. "I won't entrust the safety of my family to the Secret Service, CIA, U.S. Marshals, or anyone else. I've sacrificed myself, but I will not sacrifice my family. You managed to protect them from a highly motivated, skilled, and vengeful Mossad agent, and his two crazy team members."

"Ziv was of considerable help," Boone said.

"Yes he was," Malak said. "But you did well too. We co-opted your surveillance and you still managed to follow Angela and Q, intercept Eben, and find me." She looked down at Croc. "I assume the tracking device is in his collar."

Boone nodded.

"Clever." She looked at her watch one last time. "I have to go. Give me your word that you'll protect my family with your life."

"You have my word," Boone said.

"And that you and your team won't pass any of the intelligence I give you to any other agency unless I say it's okay."

"Done," Boone said.

"Can you arrange to have Angela and Q in D.C. tomorrow?"

"It's a little short notice," Boone said. "And Match is on a national tour."

"It's important," Malak said.

"I'll see what I can do."

"Good enough. Are your phones encrypted?"

"Yes," Boone answered. "With the latest technology. They're bullet proof."

"Nothing is bullet proof, Mr. Boone. Does anyone in the government have access to the numbers?"

"Just one person," Boone said. "And just my number."

"Potus," Malak said.

Boone nodded.

"Him we'll have to trust."

She pulled Angela into her and gave her another hug.

"I'm sorry for everything, Angela, and I wish I had more time to explain." She let Angela go and said, "I'll be in touch in a few days."

Malak Tucker, aka the Leopard, walked out of the apartment without looking back.

The three of us (four counting Croc) stood there for a few seconds staring at the empty doorway. When Dirk had left I heard every footfall on every step. Malak went down the stairs without a sound. Like a cat.

Eben walked into Carma's hotel room and found his two former team members gagged and bound together like Siamese twins. No trick knots like the boy had used on his sister.

Twins, he thought again with amazement. The idea that Malak had an identical twin had never entered Eben's mind. And he would have never believed it if he hadn't heard the girl's interview and Tyrone Boone's lengthy explanation of what he thought had happened at Independence Hall on November 30, 2004. Even after the explanation he was a little suspicious, but Boone had erased his last seeds of doubt by making a call and handing the cell phone to him. On the other end was none other than J.R. Culpepper, the president of the United States…a man not always popular in the country where he was commander in chief, but in the intelligence community he was greatly respected and known as someone with a deep understanding about what was "really" going on in the world.

He cut Carma and Devorah loose. They tore their gags off and it was a good ten minutes before their outrage subsided enough for him to talk to them.

"The leopard is dead," he began.

"How?" Carma asked.

Eben put his index finger to his temple. "A single silenced bullet."

"Where?" Devorah ask.

"At an old farmhouse outside the city."

"Why didn't you come and get us?" Carma asked.

"No time," Eben said. "When I went to the hospital I discovered that Ziv wasn't there and that his injury was greatly exaggerated. He had just left in a taxi. They told me he'd been dropped off at a car rental agency. I picked him up just as he pulled out of the parking lot and followed him to the farmhouse."

"Ziv called and said that the mission had been scrapped and we were to go home," Carma said.

"He probably made the call while I was following him," Eben said. "He infiltrated us. He worked for the leopard."

Carma and Devorah stared at him in silence. A breach of security like this was unforgivable within the Mossad.

"He could have killed any one of us anytime," Carma said.

"He could have killed all of us," Devorah said. "Why didn't he?"

"He would have gotten around to it," Eben answered. "But I think he was waiting to find out what we knew. It was my fault. I should have checked his credentials with the Institute more carefully." Eben paused. "But the point is moot. I killed him too. He and the leopard are in the same hole in the Pennsylvania woods. There's no need to put him in the report unless you want to."

Devorah and Carma shook their heads vigorously. Eben was primarily responsible for the breach, but they would be blamed as well. Their handlers would want to know how they had missed this.

"Thank you," Eben said. "I would like to leave the Institute with a clean record."

"What do you mean 'leave'?" Devorah asked.

Eben pulled the crumpled resignation letter out of his pocket. The only change he had made to it was the date. He handed it to Devorah. "This is it for me," he said. "Last mission. Not my best, but we accomplished the goal. When you get back to Tel Aviv give this to them and tell them to leave me alone." He paused. "And I'm giving the kill to you two."

"What?" Devorah and Carma asked simultaneously.

"My final report will say that the three of us followed the leopard and her male accomplice to the farm and that you took them out. There is no need to mention that the SOS team tied you up in your hotel room while I completed the mission. Since I'm leaving the Institute another successful terrorist kill will do me little good."

Devorah and Carma were visibly relieved and delighted with the scenario, as Eben knew they would be. He stood up. "I will E-mail you the final report so when you arrive in Tel Aviv tomorrow you'll be able to corroborate the story during your debriefing."

"You're not coming to Tel Aviv?" Devorah asked.

Eben shook his head. "I have friends here that I want to visit. After that I don't know what I'll do. Head off to a tropical beach, I hope."

"What about the SOS team?" Carma asked. "We have a score to even with them."

"Forget them," Eben said. "They're former intelligence agents working under private contract. Headhunters. Commission only. They were trying to beat us to the leopard." He smiled. "No payday for them this time."

Eben shook their hands solemnly, then left the hotel room. He walked two blocks down the street and climbed into an old van. X was typing on one of the keyboards, pausing only long enough to give him a nod.

"How'd it go?" Vanessa asked.

"Perfectly," Eben replied.

"I found a dentist that's willing to come in after hours and look at that cracked tooth of yours."

"Vanessa," Eben said. *"You're an angel."*

X let out a groan.

Backstage

We got to The Electric Factory just before Roger and Mom were ready to go on. We would have been there sooner, but Boone insisted that we stop at the motor coach for a quick shower and change of clothes. He said we looked like we'd been through a war. And he was right.

Mom threw her arms around me and Roger did the same to Angela.

"We were so worried when we couldn't get in touch with you," Mom said. "And then the airplane had a mechanical problem. We barely made it here in time for the concert. They were putting our makeup on in the limo. What did you do while we were gone?"

"Took in the sights, did our homework," I said. "Philadelphia is a very historic city. A lot of important things happened here."

"Two minutes!" Buddy shouted.

"Did you see *The Today Show*?" Mom asked.

"Yeah. You and Roger were great."

I looked over at Roger and Angela. They were talking while a woman was fussing with Roger's hair. I couldn't hear what they were saying above the roar of the crowd, but I was certain that Angela was giving him the same bland story that I had just given Mom. I peeked out and saw Dr. Rask and Dr. Wilson. They had center-stage seats, second row.

Boone was talking to Art and Marie over in a corner…no doubt filling them in on what they had missed.

Heather Hughes was talking to the drummer and laughing.

"One minute!" Buddy shouted.

Buddy's cell phone vibrated. He whipped it out and glanced at the screen. I thought he would ignore the call this close to show time, but he put the phone to his ear.

"Is this a joke?" he asked, then listened, and looked rattled. "Yes sir… Of course… We would be happy to… Yes… We'll leave tonight after the concert… Thank you…" He flipped the phone closed and turned to Mom. "You won't believe who that was."

"Who?" Mom asked.

"The president of the United States. He's a big fan. So are his kids. Wants us to do a show at the White House on Sunday."

"Do we have time?"

"We'll make time. Can't pass it up. We'll head down to D.C. tonight after the concert. He said he wants you and your kids to stay at the White House." He looked at his watch. "Go, band!"

The band headed out onto the stage.

Buddy positioned Mom and Roger at the entrance.

They took each other's hands.

"Now!" Buddy said.

Roger and Blaze Tucker walked out onto the stage.

A wild cheer went up.

Match began to sing.

I, Q

(Book Two: The White House)

Roland Smith

Sleeping Bear Press™

SATURDAY, SEPTEMBER 6 >

1600 Pennsylvania Avenue

Boone pulled the coach up to the back gate of the White House. It was 2:00 in the morning. While Mom and Roger packed their overnight bags in the master suite, Boone gestured me and Angela to the front of the coach.

"Buddy and the band are staying at the Willard Hotel two blocks away," he explained quietly. "I'll be at Blair House right across the street from here. It's the official residence for visiting dignitaries and heads of state. My point is that the SOS team will be close by. Not that you'll be in any danger inside the White House... It's probably the most secure building in the world."

"Why do you think my moth–" Angela stopped herself. "–Malak wanted us to come down here?"

"I'm sure she'll let us know when she's ready," Boone said. "Under no circumstances, and I mean this, are you to disable or turn off your BlackBerrys. We're past all that now. We need to know exactly where you are every second of the day from now on. Is that understood?"

Angela and I nodded.

"I'll be in constant touch with you either by phone, text message, or E-mail. And I expect you to do the same."

Again Angela and I nodded.

Roger and Mom came out of the bedroom with their bags. They were tired after their concert at the Electric Factory in Philadelphia a few hours earlier, but excited.

"Do you have everything?" Mom asked me.

I gave her a smile and showed her the small bag I was carrying.

"Let's go see the president," Roger said.

I doubted President J.R. Culpepper was going to be greeting us at 2 A.M. at the security gate. And I was right. We walked up to the gate and were met by a man and a woman dressed in business suits and big smiles on their faces. They looked like public relations people, but the earpieces in their right ears gave them away. They were with the Secret Service. I wondered if they had known Angela's mother, and if Roger and Angela were wondering the same thing.

"I'm glad you were able to make it down here on such short notice," the woman said. "You must be exhausted."

"We'll have to run you through a little security check before we let you in," the man said. "But it will only take a couple of minutes."

Uniformed White House security checked our identifications against the computer they had in the guard station, gave our bags a quick search, then ran the bags through an x-ray machine. We walked through a metal detector and were wanded after we passed through.

"You're all set to go," the man in the suit said.

"We are very excited to have you here," the woman said. "I simply love your music."

"Thank you," Mom said.

"The president has put you and Roger in the Lincoln Bedroom, on the second floor," the woman continued.

"Wow," Roger said.

"Where are Q and Angela sleeping?" Mom asked.

"They'll be up in the residential quarters," the woman said. "The bedrooms are not quite as historical, but they are very nice rooms and adjacent to each other. You can sleep in tomorrow. The president and first lady have a brunch planned for you at 11 A.M., but if you get hungry before then all you have to do is call the kitchen and they'll bring whatever you want to your rooms. The kitchen is open twenty-four hours a day."

Whatever I want, I thought. Twenty-four hours a day. I was going to pick up my phone bright and early and order a platter of food with absolutely no vegetable matter on it.

Angela and I left Mom and Roger in the Lincoln Bedroom, after a brief tour, and the woman led us to our bedrooms, which were great. I said goodnight to Angela, put on my pajamas, and crawled into the biggest and most comfortable bed I had ever slept in. I thought about testing the kitchen offer by ordering a small vanilla milkshake and an order of fries before going to sleep, but I decided to wait until I woke up.

I closed my eyes thinking that J.R. Culpepper, the most powerful man in the world, the commander in chief of the United States, Potus, was probably only a few yards away, snoring.

I fell asleep with a smile on my face, but I wasn't asleep long. I woke to a light tapping on my door. Angela had slipped into my room before I was able to sit up.

"What's the matter?" I asked groggily.

"I just got a text message from Malak," she said.

I sat up. "What'd she want?"

"See for yourself."

I turned on the light and read the short message on Angela's BlackBerry. I was suddenly wide awake and out of bed. "Did you call Boone?"

"I forwarded him the message," Angela said. "He wrote right back and said that he would be in touch."

"That's all?"

Angela nodded.

"What should we do?"

"Wait," Angela said.

We waited for half an hour, expecting Boone to call any moment, but he didn't call. Instead there was another knock on my door. I opened it.

Standing in the hallway was a very serious and alert (considering the time of morning) Secret Service agent.

"The president would like to see you both in the Oval Office," he said.

"Now?" I asked. It was 3 A.M.

He gave me a curt nod.

"Maybe we should change," I said.

"You're fine," the agent said. "He's waiting. Follow me."

Angela and I were going to meet the president of the United States in our PJs.

www.IQtheSeries.com